Nick Gifford says:

Imagine a place where all your darkest
nightmares come true.

Now imagine something far, far worse.

That's what I did.

And now I want to share it with you . . .

Nick Gifford also writes adult novels under the name Keith Brooke. As well as writing, Nick develops web sites and lives with his wife and children in north-east Essex.

Books by Nick Gifford

FLESH AND BLOOD
PIGGIES

FLESH
&
BLOOD

NICK GIFFORD

PUFFIN

PUFFIN BOOKS

Published by the Penguin Group
Penguin Books Ltd, 80 Strand, London WC2R 0RL, England
Penguin Group (USA), Inc., 375 Hudson Street, New York, New York 10014, USA
Penguin Books Australia Ltd, 250 Camberwell Road, Camberwell, Victoria 3124, Australia
Penguin Books Canada Ltd, 10 Alcorn Avenue, Toronto, Ontario, Canada M4V 3B2
Penguin Books India (P) Ltd, 11 Community Centre, Panchsheel Park, New Delhi – 110 017, India
Penguin Books (NZ) Ltd, Cnr Rosedale and Airborne Roads, Albany, Auckland, New Zealand
Penguin Books (South Africa) (Pty) Ltd, 24 Sturdee Avenue, Rosebank 2196, South Africa

Penguin Books Ltd, Registered Offices: 80 Strand, London WC2R 0RL, England

www.penguin.com

First published 2004
1

Set in Adobe Sabon
Typeset by Rowland Phototypesetting Ltd, Bury St Edmunds, Suffolk
Made and printed in England by Clays Ltd, St Ives plc

British Library Cataloguing in Publication Data
A CIP catalogue record for this book is available from the British Library

ISBN 0–141–31605–5

CONTENTS

PART FOUR – The Reckoning

PROLOGUE

Matt was lying, face down, on the beach again.

Had he escaped? Had he broken free from this awful place?

He turned on to his side and, gradually, his eyes came to focus on a pale object a short distance from his face.

Embedded in the beach was a human skull.

A jagged crack ran upwards from its left eye-socket, and crawling all over the thing were hundreds of tiny brown sand-flies.

Horrified, he looked more closely at the sand and shingle: scattered everywhere were small white fragments of bone, broken vertebrae, lost teeth.

Slowly, he swung his gaze out to sea. Dark storm clouds hung over deep red waves. It was the sea of his dreams, the sea of blood. Debris floated in the bay, and he did not want to look too closely to see what the floating objects might be. Flocks of gulls soared and swooped, feasting on the carnage, their white plumage stained a gruesome, sticky crimson.

He twisted away and threw up on the sand.

He was struggling to control his breathing, he

had to calm down. This was no longer a dream, he was actually *here* . . .

He made himself look around again. He had to get out of here, but how do you wake yourself from a dream that has entirely swallowed you up?

There was an old tramp a short distance away, shuffling along the tideline, turning over the jetsam with the open toe of one of his boots. Matt wondered what he was hoping to find.

His senses were becoming numbed to all the horrors that he was seeing, he realized. Even when the tramp squatted down to extract something from a dark, tangled mass, Matt didn't look away. Even when the tramp raised his trophy to his mouth and bit into it.

Matt struggled to his feet. He climbed the concrete steps to the Promenade and was surprised to see how many holidaymakers were here, despite the deep gloom of the weather. He stopped himself, suddenly frightened at how easy it was to accept this grim distortion as reality: a world of holidays and football and school and work, a world where nothing was really any different.

The people were dressed in a strange assortment of clothing, as if they had all taken part in a lucky dip at some monstrous jumble sale. Striped blazers, frilly summer frocks with parasols, mismatched items of school uniform, pin-striped trousers with torn T-shirts, patchwork waistcoats, wide-brimmed straw hats, long leather coats, high boots, fur caps.

Couples strolled, arm in arm, their faces pale

and hollowed out, as if they were being eaten away from within. Emaciated dogs tottered along after their grotesquely overweight owners. Tiny children, covered only in dark-red mud from the beach, chased each other through the crowds, while others gathered around an ice-cream vendor's stall.

And all the time, as Matt walked along the Prom, eyes followed him, tracking his progress. Even the children stopped what they were doing to stare.

They all knew that he didn't belong here, that he was new in this terrible place. He understood now that this was another world: a world constructed from the darker shadows of the one he knew.

All the time, the eyes followed him.

He kept walking, fearful of what might happen if he stood still for too long.

It had all started with Gran's funeral, he supposed: that fateful visit to the family home in Crooked Elms. Or perhaps it went back further than that.

He had to think his situation through. He had to work out how to get out of here. There had to be a way!

The alternative was too awful to consider.

PART ONE
LIFE AND DEATH

1

A FAMILY
GATHERING

Matt Guilder stared at the composed features of
his grandmother. They had made up her face so
that her skin was smooth, the wrinkles eased away.
He had never known Gran well but he remembered
her as far older than this.

He couldn't stop staring. At any moment he
expected her to turn and look at him.

A hand squeezed his arm. His father: strong,
reassuring, just a little impatient. 'Come on, boy,' he
said. 'You're causing a traffic jam.'

Matt made himself turn away from his dead
grandmother. He and his father left the room as
others filed in to pay their last respects.

They walked back through to the front room of
his grandparents' house, to where his mother and
her sister Carol were sitting either side of Gramps.
Matt sat down by his mother but she barely noticed
him. His father went and stood with Uncle Mike
by the window, saying nothing, just staring across
the paddock to the church and the woods beyond.

There were about a dozen people in the room:
members of the family, many of whom Matt barely

recognized; most of his mother's side of the family were strangers to him. He had only ever met them on one or two awkward family occasions. He sat in silence, waiting for something to happen.

No matter how hard he tried, he couldn't get that scene out of his head: Gran, lying in her open coffin in the room she had called the library, floral tributes arranged all around her.

It was the look on her face that stuck in his mind. Her expression wasn't quite the blank look you might expect from a corpse. There had been an inquest after her death, and it had heard that she had fallen down the stairs after her fatal heart attack; but there was no sign of injury now, so that was not what was bothering him. There was something else, something more. It was as if she were trying to tell them something from beyond death.

And then he realized what it was: she looked *relieved*. As if death had offered her some kind of refuge. He tried to swallow the sudden dry lump in his throat.

There was a noise from the hallway. The undertakers had arrived to seal Gran into her coffin and take her on the short journey to the village church.

Matt walked to the church with his father and Uncle Mike, the three of them slightly apart from the rest of the procession.

'How was the trip?' asked Uncle Mike, a short, shuffling man whose every gesture seemed to apologize for his very existence.

'Busy,' said Matt, when it seemed that his father couldn't be bothered to summon up the effort to reply.

'Nah,' said his father dismissively. 'You should try the M25 – *that's* busy.'

His father was a photocopier salesman. He drove over a thousand miles a week.

Matt stared at the ground as his father went on, 'What a way to spend a Tuesday morning, eh, Mike?'

Uncle Mike grunted. 'Sure,' he said. 'I tell you, I could have done without all this. The old bag always hated me, anyway.'

Matt's father gave a short laugh, then he caught Matt's eye and stopped. 'Maybe, Mike,' he said. 'But she wasn't all bad.'

Matt looked away again. His father had said almost exactly the same as Mike only the previous evening. His parents had been arguing, as they usually did before they had to go anywhere together. 'She always hated me,' his father had said at one point. 'They all did!' It had suddenly given Matt a different perspective on his parents: what they must have been like before he had come along, before they were married. It must have been hard for his father – the brash young salesman from London – to break into this close-knit rural family. He must have tried hard to win the approval of Gran and Gramps, but he had never really succeeded. In the end he had given up trying. It was a side of his father that Matt had never even guessed at before.

'Not all bad?' Mike echoed, in answer to Matt's father's platitudes. 'She made a pretty good show of it then.'

Matt was surprised how many people had come to fill the church. It seemed that all of the village had turned out to send his grandmother on her way. History, he supposed: the Wareden family went back generations in the village of Crooked Elms.

The vicar was young and nervous-looking. Matt recognized him from the house, although at the time he had taken him for a distant cousin, perhaps. How could he have missed the dog collar, he wondered. The vicar had thick glasses and a patchy blond beard that he didn't really seem old enough to be growing.

'Jesus said, I am the resurrection, and I am the life; he who believes in me, though he die, yet shall he live, and whoever lives and believes in me shall never die.' The young vicar sounded like an English teacher reciting poetry, his voice somehow detached from the words, putting emphasis in all the wrong places.

Already Aunt Carol was choking back her tears in the front row, clutching her two daughters, Tina and Kirsty, to either side. Matt's mother was gripping his father's arm, her face even blanker than Gran's had been in her coffin.

Gramps stood straight, immediately in front of Matt. He'd never been an army man – he'd been a conscientious objector in the war – but now it was as if he were standing on parade. Being inspected by a senior officer.

When the funeral service was over, they filed out behind the coffin into the spring drizzle. Matt pulled his borrowed jacket tight, envying his cousin Vince his black leather jacket.

Row upon row of crooked gravestones were crammed together in the churchyard. Most were old, their edges softened by centuries of weathering, their surfaces stained and encrusted with yellow and grey discs of lichen. Here and there a few limp bunches of spring flowers brightened the gloom: offerings to the dead – as if the dead were going to notice, Matt thought dismissively.

They waited by the lychgate as the pall-bearers eased the coffin into the back of the hearse, ready to take Gran to the crematorium.

'Hope they don't drop it,' Matt's father muttered.

Matt stifled an awkward giggle, while his mother turned an angry glare on her husband.

As he stood by the lychgate, Matt noticed a small area off to one side that was separated from the rest of the churchyard by a low, wrought-iron fence. Within the fence was a single stone cross bearing the date 1898. Lined up in front of the cross were six narrow, rectangular slabs, all overgrown with brambles and yellowed grass. It was the neglected state of this patch that had caught his attention – why would nobody in the village keep that patch tidy?

Curious, Matt wandered across for a closer look.

1898. He wondered what could have happened, all that time ago. There must have been some kind of accident, he thought. Six deaths. Such a tragedy must have had a huge impact on the village.

He peered at one of the six slabs. There were words engraved on the stone. Names. The letters were hard to make out, but clearly there were four names on this slab alone, each with the same surname – something like Sapsford or Sapeford. This slab marked a family grave then.

Six slabs . . . so *six* family graves.

What could have caused such a tragedy?

Matt turned away from the disturbing monument. His grandmother's coffin was in the hearse now, and the crowd was starting to break up. He hurried to catch up with his family.

Outside his grandparents' house in the village of Crooked Elms, Matt sat alone in the back of the Volvo. On the journey back from the crematorium his parents had not exchanged a single word. Arriving here at the house, they had gone straight inside, but Matt had lingered in the car, saying he would follow them. Here, amid the clutter of his father's work, he felt safe. He thought of home. He should have been playing football for the Under-16s this morning. He wondered how the team had done.

He yawned. It was barely noon, yet it felt like the day should be nearly over.

He would have to go inside, he knew, but there was something nagging away at him that made him hold back. It would be so easy just to stay here, pretend to have dozed off. Why did days like this always last so long?

He opened the car door and climbed out. He couldn't stay here all day. He didn't want to upset his mother, or make his father angry. He didn't want to make them argue again.

His grandparents – just Gramps now, he reminded himself – lived in a large stone house that had, at various times, served the village as school-house, chapel and, more recently, doctor's surgery, until Gramps' retirement. Matt headed around the side of the house and went in by the back door.

The heat was intense after the chill spring air, and Matt suddenly felt dizzy. He leant one shoulder against a wall and surveyed the packed living room. Tables had been set out with food and drinks and there was a tight knot of people gathered around them.

Matt slipped the jacket off his shoulders and dumped it on a chair in the hallway, stepping sharply out of the way as Aunt Carol rushed by with another plateful of sandwiches. As she plunged through the living room, the throng parted before her as if she were somehow projecting her presence in front of her. She was that kind of woman, he supposed. You always knew she was there.

He still felt hot and a little dizzy. He loosened his black tie, then rubbed at his eyes.

His mouth felt dry, so he entered the living-room and joined the congestion around the tables. Instantly, a paper plate was thrust at him by small hands.

His eyes followed the hands, the thin arms buried in a sombre black-and-purple dress, and met the blank look of his young cousin, Kirsty. She pushed the plate at him until he took it, then followed up with a serviette.

He nodded. 'Thanks, Kirsty,' he said. She clearly had no idea who he was.

As ever, Tina was by her side. At twelve, she was five years older than Kirsty, but, other than the difference in size, they could have been twins. Both had mid-brown hair tied hard back from their faces, and both wore wire-framed glasses that only served to emphasize the squint they had inherited from their father.

'This is cousin Matthew,' said Tina, tipping her head so that her mouth was close to her sister's ear. 'He's with Aunty Jill and Uncle Nigel. They're from Norwich, Norfolk.'

At each of these statements, Kirsty nodded solemnly. 'Pleased to meet you, cousin Matthew,' she said finally. Tina patted her sister's arm approvingly.

Matt turned away. There were drinks on the table. He glanced around, then took a dainty glass of sherry. He took a sip, and it was sweet and thick and clung to the lining of his throat as he tried to swallow. He put his glass and plate down. He felt hot and dizzy again, and he had to clutch at the mantelpiece for support.

It was this place, he decided: the dry, dusty atmosphere, the heat of all these bodies crowded together. All the voices seemed to be swirling around him and, as he stood there, he suddenly experienced a most vivid flashback to when he was a small child, sitting in his father's arms on a roundabout in a park, the world spinning around him as if it would never stop . . . never stop . . . never . . .

Matt struggled to swallow again. He could feel the heat threatening to smother him, hear the voices start to echo around his head once more. Maybe he was going down with something.

Just then there was a sudden cry. Matt turned, to see a commotion around the food tables.

'It's all right, it's all right,' said Carol, sweeping through the crowd.

Kirsty was lying on the floor, her head propped up on her sister's lap. 'Mother,' said Tina matter-of-factly. 'It's OK. Kirsty has just had one of her turns.'

Carol took a paper plate and used it to fan her youngest child. Soon Kirsty was pushing herself up on her elbows and peering around. Her face was pale and her eyes brimming with tears behind her glasses. She looked as if she didn't know where she was.

'It's all right, darling,' said Carol. Kirsty started to sob, and buried her face in her mother's chest.

Matt turned away, wishing again that the day

would soon be over. He was intensely aware of all the people milling around: they all seemed to be eyeing the ornaments and the pictures on the walls. All these valuables ... something would have to be done with them when Gramps' turn came. It was as if everybody was making a mental list, staking their claims in advance.

Gramps was sitting in a high-backed armchair by the far fireplace.

Matt felt compelled to approach him, despite the heat pouring out of the fire. He caught his mother's eye and smiled. She was standing just behind Gramps, as if she could bring herself neither to sit with him nor leave him alone.

He leant over and touched his grandfather's arm. 'Hi, Gramps,' he said.

The pale blue eyes stared past him, their gaze fixed on some distant point.

Matt sat on a footstool and looked in the same direction. Gramps was gazing out of the window, across the paddock to the church and the woods. He turned towards Matt. 'Matthew,' he said, and he smiled. 'I'm glad you came, boy. You all right, are you? Look a bit off-colour.'

'You should know,' said Matt. 'You're the doc.'

Gramps smiled, his gaze becoming distant once again.

The heat by the fire was quite intense. Matt could feel his shirt starting to stick to his back.

'. . . burning now.'

The word *burning* jerked Matt back to awareness.

16

He'd been drifting again. He saw his mother's sudden look of concern, and he mumbled, 'Hmm?'

'Dorothea,' said Gramps. 'She'll be burning now. Or they'll have done it already.'

Suddenly Matt realized what he was talking about: Gran's cremation.

'It's right, of course,' said Gramps, as if he were merely talking about the weather. 'We Waredens always burn, one way or another. The only way to end up is as ashes – there's nothing they can do with ashes. It's the best way.'

'Dad,' said Matt's mother, leaning down over his chair.

Matt saw how his grandfather's knuckles had whitened as his grip on the arms of his chair had intensified.

'Ashes to ashes,' Gramps recited in a weak, croaking voice. 'Dust to dust . . . all gone to dust . . . they make glue from the bones of horses – that'd be all right, too. There's no way back from glue.'

Matt tipped back in his seat as his mother moved round to calm Gramps. The old man was rocking back and forth in his chair as he rambled, and every word forced spit and bubbles out past his yellowed teeth.

'Ashes,' he gasped. 'Ashes.' Over and over, all he would say was, 'Ashes.'

When Matt stood up, he felt dizzy again. He was losing track of what was going on: had Gramps really started to rant and ramble like that, or was it all happening in Matt's head?

He staggered away, barging into people as he went.

All he could hear was Gramps saying, 'Ashes, ashes, she's gone to ashes.'

Round and round in his head.

It felt like he was on that roundabout again, the voices spinning round, the ground shifting beneath his feet.

He tugged at his tie, desperate for air.

The doorway.

He was in the hall. Cooler here. He heard his father laughing, saying something about too much sherry. He didn't care – let them laugh, let them talk about ashes and sherry and whatever else it was that they were talking about.

He reached the front door, swung it open and breathed in deeply.

It was as if someone had just turned on all the lights: the sudden blast of clarity as he sucked cold air deep into his lungs.

There was a U-shaped drive at the front of the house, and now it was packed, nose to tail, with cars, with yet more lining the narrow street.

He started to breathe more steadily now, starting to recover his self-control.

He had panicked in there: the heat, the mad ramblings of his grandfather . . . it had all been too much for him.

He wasn't alone out here, he suddenly realized.

Sitting on the bonnet of an old Ford Escort, bottle of wine in one hand, cigarette in the other, was

Vince. He was about nineteen, tall and thin with dyed black hair and pale features. He had a strange way of staring at people, and no one with any sense would meet his look for long. Matt suspected that a lot of it was an act – but it was pretty effective, all the same. His cousin was watching him now, grinning. He took a long drag on his cigarette and puffed a perfect blue-grey O into the spring air.

Matt nodded at him, wondering if he should go back inside.

'You look like you've seen her ghost,' said Vince.

Matt shrugged. 'Had all I could take,' he said. 'I didn't know you were out here.'

Vince leant back against the windscreen and poured some wine into his mouth.

'They all in there, are they?' he demanded suddenly. 'Picking over the remains?'

Matt nodded. 'Like vultures,' he said. 'Valuing the paintings, measuring up for carpets.'

Vince laughed. 'Have they started to fight yet?' he asked. 'They always end up cracking up and fighting. Guarantee it.'

'Kirsty fainted,' said Matt. 'Gramps starting ranting. No fights yet, though.'

Vince nodded. 'Bunch of nutcases,' he said. 'Give 'em half a chance and they'll make you just like *they* are: nutcases.' He took a deep pull at his cigarette, held it in for long seconds, then blew the smoke out through his nose. 'Damn 'em all,' he said finally. 'That's what I say: damn 'em all! Let 'em all burn in hell.'

Matt turned away. He had suddenly decided he didn't want to hear any more of this.

But Vince went on, regardless. 'Mad as hatters!' he laughed. 'The curse of the Waredens, ha ha!'

PART TWO
THE WAY

2

BATHSIDE

'See you, then.'

His father was in the driver's seat of the Volvo, shirt-sleeves rolled up against the July heat. He glanced up. 'Hmm?' he grunted. 'Oh, sure. See you, Matt.'

'We're off to Bathside – remember? Mum and me. Going to the seaside to visit Gramps.'

His father was still peering into the open briefcase on his lap. 'Sure,' he said darkly. 'I remember, all right.'

At last he snapped his briefcase shut and swung it on to the passenger seat, then he looked up at Matt. 'You take care, all right?' he said. Then he smiled cruelly and added, 'And don't forget to give them all my love.'

'You'll call in, won't you? If you're passing.' For some reason, Matt wanted to prolong this moment.

His father shrugged. 'Who knows?'

Then he put the car into gear and swung out into the road, steering one-handed as he yanked his seat-belt across his chest. Matt stared after the car until all that lingered was the bad eggs smell from its catalytic converter.

It took them an hour and a half to get to Bathside by train, and Matt and his mother scarcely spoke for the entire journey. Then, just before they reached the station, he noticed his mother watching him.

'He's not well, you know,' she said uncertainly. 'Gramps is an old man. That's why he's staying with Carol – he couldn't cope on his own. It was Gran who kept him going.'

Matt nodded.

'I just want you to be prepared,' she went on. 'When someone as old as Gramps loses their independence, they sometimes ... well, sometimes they lose touch.'

There was a taxi office just across the street from Bathside station. Matt waited outside with the bags while his mother went in and arranged a ride. Soon she emerged, accompanied by an overweight man in his fifties who took the bags without a word and went round to put them in the boot of an old Toyota.

Matt sat in the back as the cab swung out into a street lined with shops.

After a journey lasting a few minutes, the taxi stopped in front of a row of terraced houses. This didn't look like the street where Aunt Carol lived . . .

Outside, Matt looked at his mother, waiting for her to explain. She pointed towards one of the houses and said, 'That's us.'

Matt followed her gesture. A wrought-iron name-plate told him that the house was called *The Gullery*, and a board in the window said:

FAMILY BED & BREAKFAST
NO PETS / SMOKING
NO VACANCIES

'It's all right,' his mother said, smiling awkwardly. 'Mrs Eldridge is expecting us – we've booked.' She reached for the bags, but Matt stopped her.

'Why?' he said. 'I thought we were staying with Aunt Carol.'

She shook her head. 'Carol's already got her hands full with Gramps and her three,' she said. 'And anyway, I think we should start as we mean to go on.'

Mrs Eldridge was about the same age as Matt's mother: fortyish, plump, with permed black hair and tiny eyes set in a round, full-moon face.

'Ah, Mrs Guilder!' she said, backing into a dark hallway. 'Come in, come in. Your rooms are ready for you. This your son, Matthew? My, my. Here, let me take those.' With that, she took the bags and set off up the steep stairs.

Matt sidestepped a toddler's plastic tricycle and followed the two women upstairs. What did his mother mean by that, he wondered. *Start as we mean to go on.*

'It's a full house this week,' said Mrs Eldridge. 'A

25

full house: we've got a young couple from Bedford and Mr Cranston on the first floor. He's a regular, Mr Cranston – last week of July every year. He's a dear, Mr Cranston. Always pays in advance. Bathroom's here' – she indicated a door marked BATHROOM – 'and your toilet's upstairs.'

The top floor held two bedrooms and a toilet that was so small you could only just get its door open.

'Thank you, Mrs Eldridge, I'm sure it'll be very comfortable,' said his mother.

Their landlady left them standing in one of the bedrooms.

His mother turned around, sweeping the sandy blonde hair out of her eyes. 'What do you reckon?' she asked. 'Which room do you want?'

Matt crossed the landing. Both rooms had twin beds covered with beige candlewick counterpanes, and a chair and dressing table made from dark, polished wood. The wallpaper was flowery and browned with age, the net curtains a grubby off-white.

'Hard to choose,' said Matt, over his shoulder. His mother was still in the other room, so Matt dumped his bag on the chair and went across to the window. Through the net curtains he could see across the street to an identical terraced row. Maybe a third of the houses in this street were Bed-and-Breakfasts, he estimated.

They probably all had the same wallpaper, too.

*

Carol met them at the door with a hug that took in both Matt and his mother. 'Darlings, darlings,' she said. 'Come in.'

They lived in an old guest-house near the sea-front at Bathside. Carol showed them into the front room, sweeping through before them to turn off the TV. Tina and Kirsty were sitting together on a long, black velveteen sofa. Until their mother interrupted them they had been playing a computer game, but they didn't complain, they just put their handsets down on a coffee table and rose to greet the visitors.

'Tina, Kirsty, they're here,' said Carol, somewhat unnecessarily.

The two girls peered through their glasses at Matt and allowed themselves to be kissed by their aunt.

'How was your journey down?' asked Carol. 'Would you like a drink? We have tea in the afternoons – I find it so refreshing in this heat, don't you? Earl Grey or Darjeeling? Tina, go and click the kettle, be a dear. I've filled it, I'll be through to pour in a minute.'

Tina turned and made for the door, shadowed by her younger sister.

Matt sat down in an armchair, his aunt's voice fast becoming a mere background noise.

A little later, Carol seemed to notice him sitting there. 'Girls,' she said, 'why don't you take cousin Matthew to see the beach, while Aunty Jill and I catch up?'

Matt glanced at Tina and Kirsty just in time to see a look pass between them: a strangely mature look, as if they were recognizing that they shared a burden.

He walked with Tina and Kirsty to the end of the road and waited for a gap in the traffic so they could cross to the Promenade.

They passed the memorial, a white six-sided block, taller than Matt, standing on a grassy island where the road forked at the top of the Prom. Each face of the block was inscribed with a long list of names, detailing the town's men lost in both World Wars.

Matt paused and looked at the bottom of the list: there were two Waredens named. Clearly, Gramps' refusal to join up had not been a family thing. Matt wondered what he would have done in such a situation. Had it taken more courage to go to war, or to be a conscientious objector, he wondered. You never know your own courage until it is tested, he supposed. Many people must pass an entire lifetime without ever facing such a test.

His cousins were waiting for him across the road.

The Prom was below them, at the foot of a steep, grassy slope. People lay on the grass, while others walked with dogs or chased around on bikes. The tide was high, the water a muddy grey, lapping meekly at the concrete flood walls. A series of stone groynes reached out into the bay, and groups of children had gone out along them to dive from their ends.

His cousins were watching him as he looked down towards the bay. It was quite startling how alike the two girls were, despite the years between them.

'Finished school for the summer?' he asked awkwardly.

Kirsty looked away, leaving her older sister to reply.

'Yesterday was our last day,' Tina said solemnly.

They headed down one of the zigzag paths that led to the Promenade. Matt could smell the salt on the air now. 'I've always liked the sea,' he said. 'Do you like living here?'

Kirsty nodded but stopped at a sharp look from her sister.

Tina said, 'The sea is a wild place. Nothing can tame the sea. Nothing can beat it back. We like it.' She paused, then asked Matt, 'Do you like living in Norwich?'

'It's OK,' he said.

'Are you going back soon?'

He looked up, surprised by her sudden pointed tone. 'I . . . yes, I expect so,' he said. 'We've just come to see Gramps. And you, of course.'

There was a perceptible lifting of tension as Tina allowed herself to smile.

She took Matt's arm – her fingers cold and sharp, like the claws of a bird – and led him across the Prom to the flood barrier. 'It's so nice to have visitors,' she said, her voice far less strained than before. 'Do you think you might be going back to Norwich *tomorrow*?'

'Oh yes, we were in Yugoslavia. 1938, I think. Stayed in Split first of all – I had to show your mother what was left of Diocletian's Palace. Then we went down the Adriatic to Dubrovnik to stay with a chap I met at Bart's. Georgios Constantine was his name. Fine doctor. Killed at Tobruk in '42. Can't remember which side he was on, the fool.'

Gramps was sitting in an armchair, a glass of sherry in one hand, the other clutching his walking stick. His face was flushed, his eyes distant as he relived one of his Mediterranean jaunts. As a young man he had travelled widely. Matt's mother sat on the sofa, leaning forward. She'd probably heard this tale a dozen times but she was smiling, encouraging her father to go on.

Matt caught her eye as he entered the room, and he couldn't help smiling too. Gramps seemed fine.

Just then his grandfather looked up. 'Well, if it isn't that young Matthew Guilder – although not so young any more. Fourteen, are you?'

'Fifteen.' Just.

Gramps nodded. 'Good to see you, my boy. You look the spitting image of your father, not that that's your fault, of course.' He chuckled at his own joke, then continued, 'I was just telling your mother . . .'

And then his expression faltered as he struggled to recall.

'Yugoslavia,' Matt's mother said gently. '1938. Your honeymoon.'

'I know, I know!' he snapped. 'I know what I was talking about, don't I, girl? You always did butt in.'

He had puffed himself up with this sudden outburst and now he let himself slowly subside, slumping back into his seat. He opened his mouth to speak, but nothing came out. Matt wasn't sure whether he was sulking at the interruption or if he had lost track again. He was still sitting like that, slumped in his chair with his mouth open, when Carol and Kirsty appeared in the doorway.

'We eat at six sharp during the week,' Carol said. 'Would you like to come through now?'

Kirsty took Gramps' hand and helped him to stand. It was the first time Matt had seen her do anything independently of Tina.

He followed them through to the dining room.

A long, rectangular, pine table had been laid out for dinner, with cutlery, cane place mats, up-turned wine glasses and neatly folded paper serviettes at each place. Matt couldn't help recalling the funeral once again: Carol rushing about with the food, Tina and Kirsty handing out paper plates and serviettes.

Carol guided him through to sit at the far side of the table, next to Gramps. Beyond his grandfather, Kirsty perched on a stool she had brought in from the kitchen. It was cramped at the table, with barely room for the eight place-settings.

There was a serving hatch in the far wall, and Matt could see through into the kitchen. Tina was

31

filling serving dishes with something from the cooker, while her mother fussed at something in the sink. Occasionally they exchanged a few muttered words and Aunt Carol would step to the kitchen door and peer out along the hallway.

Matt glanced at his mother. She was staring down at her place mat, a blank, polite look on her face.

Kirsty was leaning against her grandfather's arm, humming a tune Matt half recognized but couldn't quite place. Gramps was staring through the serving hatch with an unseeing look, his mouth still open a little way as if he was about to speak.

After a few minutes, Carol came into the room. 'Apologies,' she said through a brittle, forced smile. 'I misjudged the timing.'

She put a long silver dish of new potatoes on a mat in the centre of the table, then stepped aside as Tina brought in a dish of peas, French beans and baby carrots.

Aunt Carol glanced over her shoulder again, then said, 'I'm afraid Vincent and Uncle Mike haven't returned from work yet. Apologies, again. I *told* them six o'clock.'

She went back into the kitchen and moments later returned with three plates, each with a piece of baked fish arranged in the middle. Tina brought the remaining three plates, two with fish and one with some sort of nut roast for Gramps.

'Do start, please,' said Carol, spooning some potatoes on to her father's plate.

*

Matt had nearly finished when Uncle Mike appeared. He shuffled into the doorway and stopped abruptly at the sight of the meal in progress. He squinted at the brass clock on the sideboard, then raised a hand to his face in an apologetic gesture.

'Carol, love,' he said. 'Sorry. Really, I'm sorry. I was held up. Stuck at the office with the VAT man.'

Carol glowered at her husband over a half-raised fork. Slowly, she lowered the fork. Then she smiled. 'Michael,' she said. 'Aren't you going to say hello to Jill and Matthew?' All the time she spoke, her smile never faltered.

Mike looked at Carol and Matt. He still hadn't moved from the doorway. He nodded. 'Evening,' he said. 'How was the journey down?'

'Fine,' Matt's mother said awkwardly.

Tina came in with her father's plate of fish. Matt hadn't noticed her slipping through to the kitchen to get it.

Uncle Mike came to sit next to Matt. He smelt of beer and cigarettes. He must have had his meeting with the VAT man in a pub.

Mike picked at the fish, all the time under the relentless gaze of his wife. 'Where's Vince?' he asked, after a time.

Carol looked at the clock, then shook her head. 'That boy,' she said. 'I told him six o'clock.'

Tina and her mother removed the plates and the empty vegetable dishes. There was apple pie and cream for dessert. 'Tina made it all herself,' Carol said proudly.

'It looks lovely,' said Matt's mother.

They ate in awkward silence. Just as they were finishing, the front door thumped shut.

'What are you all gawping at?' demanded Vince as he appeared in the doorway where his father had stood, only twenty minutes earlier.

'Vincent,' said Aunt Carol in a warning tone.

He looked around the room blankly. 'Yeah?' he said.

'Your mother told you six o'clock,' said Uncle Mike, as if he himself had been there all along.

'Yeah?' said Vince. 'And I said, "Maybe." OK?'

Mike had turned in his chair, so that Matt could no longer see the expression on his face. His ears were bright red, though. He was angry. Probably very angry indeed.

Finally Mike said in a low voice, 'Aren't you going to say hello to Jill and Matt? They've come visiting.'

Vince shrugged. 'I've got eyes in my head, haven't I?' he said. He nodded in the general direction of his aunt.

All the time this had been going on, Matt had been aware of a sudden tension in his grandfather's posture. Gramps was staring at Vince. Tina and Kirsty were staring, too.

Vince returned all the hostile looks, then shook his head. 'I don't have to take this,' he said, backing into the hall. 'It's like living in an asylum, this is.'

Seconds later, the front door opened and then

thumped shut. There was the sound of a car door slamming, an engine revving, a squeal of tyres.

Matt looked round the room. Gramps and his mother were staring blankly at the table again. Mike and Carol were glaring at each other. And the girls were sitting upright, smiling weakly.

Carol straightened, and the brittle smile forced itself on to her face again.

'Something to drink?' she said brightly. 'We drink coffee after dinner in this family – I always feel it clears the palate after a good meal, don't you? Father? Jill? Matthew?'

3

DEAD AND BURIED

He's in a corridor. Brick walls rise up all around him, a corrugated-tin roof closes in over his head. A dark gutter runs along the centre of the concrete floor.

The heat is intense, the stench almost over-powering.

He keeps going, turns another corner. The dark corridor stretches out ahead of him, more brick walls to either side. As he runs, he feels his feet sticking to the ground, pulling him back as if he's running through mud.

The smell is coming from something dead, he realizes. Putrefying flesh.

And it's following him . . . *catching up* with him.

A junction. He guesses left, feels something in his head shifting, as if he is somehow mentally aware of some abominable presence not far behind him.

His chest is aching, each breath a desperate effort. His feet feel like lead weights.

He reaches another junction, swings round the corner and –

*

Matt sat up straight in his bed, his T-shirt stuck to his body, his chest aching as he gasped for just one more breath . . .

He peered around the room, the shadows and dark shapes now familiar. He resisted the strong impulse to reach for the cord above his bed and flood the room with light.

He pulled his T-shirt up over his head and tossed it on to the floor, then lay back. He was sick of Bathside. Sick of long, empty days in an unfamiliar town.

They had been here for eight days now: more than long enough to see Gramps. More than long enough for Aunt Carol's forced welcome to wear thin. More than long enough to do all they had to do.

He had phoned friends in Norwich a few times, but that hadn't helped. They just thought he was on holiday, they didn't realize how awful it was to be stuck in a drab seaside town with family who didn't really want you around.

Yesterday he had called home for the second time but, just as before, he only reached the answering machine: 'Hi, Nigel Guilder here – all your copying and reprographic requirements satisfied with the minimum of fuss. Afraid I can't make it to the phone right now, but if you'd be so good as to leave your number after the tone I'll get back to you at the first opportunity. Thanks for calling.'

Matt hadn't left a message. He suspected his father was making the most of his freedom – he would hardly want Matt bothering him with how boring a time he was having.

He wondered if his mother had tried to get through at all. He thought that she probably hadn't, and he didn't like that thought.

It was starting to get light now. Perhaps he should just stay awake until morning. Perhaps . . .

In the morning, Matt went with his mother to visit Gran's grave.

They drove out to Crooked Elms in the back of a taxi, a rare extravagance on his mother's part – she was so careful with money these days. She'd never been like that, back in Norwich.

'If Dad was here, we could have gone in the Volvo,' said Matt, sullenly.

His mother pushed a strand of hair away from her eyes and opened her mouth to speak but then stopped herself. His words had clearly hurt her and he wasn't sure whether it was satisfaction he felt, or guilt.

She started again. 'Dad's working,' she said. 'We can't always rely on your father.'

When they left the taxi, they followed a gravel path through the crowded graveyard and around the side of the church. The grass between the haphazard rows of headstones had recently been mown, and its sweet smell was heavy in the air.

The grounds to the rear of the church were less crowded, the stones cleaner, sharper-edged, more recent.

Gran didn't have a headstone. Instead, she had a small plaque set at the foot of a high stone wall. It carried her name and the dates of her birth and death, nothing else.

His mother was kneeling before the plaque, her pale blue eyes unfocused, distant. Matt stayed at her side for a minute or two, then turned away. Let her be alone, he thought. Give her some peace.

The small path wound around the back of the church and then joined another, wider track. To his right, the track led through a kissing gate towards the dark shade of Copperas Wood. He turned left, heading back towards the front of the church.

As soon as he saw the low, wrought-iron fence he remembered it from Gran's funeral: the mass grave from some time late in the nineteenth century.

He went closer and saw the year '1898' engraved on the tall stone cross at the back of the small enclosure. He peered through the brambles and tall grass to read the stone slabs which covered each of the six family graves.

Four members of the Sapsford family. Three members of the Johnsons. Four Todd-Martins.

'Twenty-one dead, from six families.'

Matt jumped at the sudden voice behind him. He turned and squinted in the harsh sunlight. A young man, blond, glasses, patchy beard. It was the vicar who had conducted Gran's funeral service.

Matt relaxed a little. 'I noticed it before,' he said, feeling a need to justify his curiosity. 'Were they all from the village?'

The vicar nodded. 'A tragic loss,' he said. 'It's hard to put yourself in the position of those who had to endure such a catastrophe.'

'What happened?'

The vicar spread his hands in a gesture of help-lessness. 'There was a madness in this place,' he said mysteriously. 'A single night of quite horrific violence, and six families were destroyed and an entire village left in shock. Accounts from the time are confused and unclear.

'I asked the same questions when I came to this parish six years ago. My predecessor was somewhat old-fashioned: he laid the blame on the Devil.'

Matt suppressed a shiver. 'Is that why nobody looks after this part of the churchyard?' he asked, waving a hand at the tangle of brambles which covered the enclosure.

'People are scared,' said the vicar. 'Scared of the madness, scared of what happened that night. Each of us has something of the Devil within us: no one will work here because it reminds them of this fact.'

All the way back to Bathside, sitting on the top deck of the bus, those words kept coming back to Matt: *each of us has something of the Devil within us*. It sounded like something out of the Dark Ages.

Vicars these days were supposed to be modern, to wear jeans and play tambourines. What must it have taken to make the young vicar of Crooked Elms talk so readily of the Devil like that?

4

THE OUTSIDER

They were talking about the possibility of selling the family house at Crooked Elms. Carol and Matt's mother were in the kitchen, with the windows wide open. Matt sat in the shady part of the garden, staring at the pages of a thriller, unable to focus.

'Mike says it's the best option,' said Carol. 'He says it should raise at least a quarter of a million.'

Matt couldn't see his mother's expression, but from the long silence he could picture it clearly: eyes down, lower lip sucked in, reaching up to push the hair away from her eyes. When she spoke, the tone of her voice told him he had been right. 'I don't know,' she said hesitantly. 'It seems so . . . so *tacky*: that we should be talking like this behind his back. Have you spoken to Dad about it?'

'He didn't understand,' said Carol in a strained tone. 'He didn't even know which house I was talking about.'

'Can't we wait?'

'It's expensive, Jill, darling.' Carol had adopted a patient tone now, the one she used on her father when he was at his least cooperative. 'I'm running two households here on a single budget. Dad's pension barely meets his drinks bill. I've tried to reason with him, but he's as stubborn as me.'

'But that house has been in the family for generations,' Matt's mother said. 'There have always been Waredens in Crooked Elms.'

'We sell it now,' Carol said harshly. 'Or we sell it when Dad's passed away. That's the truth of the matter. I never liked that place, anyway.'

That afternoon, Matt wandered back into town. This was how his days were spent: walking from place to place, sitting around reading, just waiting while time passed. He didn't belong here. He didn't fit in. It all seemed so pointless . . .

Eventually he ended up at the Bed-and-Breakfast. He let himself into the house and climbed the stairs, a heavy feeling of gloom descending with each step.

He pushed at his door, went in and looked around.

Everything was in its place: his books lined up on the dressing table, along with his comb and washing bag. His dirty jeans were slumped in the corner where he had dropped them the night before last. His signed picture of Michael Owen was still Blu-tacked to the back of the door. There was an old crisp packet in the bin and the sticky stain of spilt Coke on his bedside table – Mrs Eldridge clearly had not been in to clean up today.

So why did he suddenly feel as if his space had been violated? Why did his eyes keep skipping round the room as if he was expecting someone to jump out from some hidden crevice?

He went downstairs again. Somehow he didn't find the prospect of filling time in his room very appealing any more.

He met Mrs Eldridge in the hallway, emerging from the front room with a pile of ironing up to her chin.

'Oh, Matt,' she said. 'I didn't know you were back. Still enjoying the seaside, are you?'

'Sure,' he said. 'Great.'

'Good, good.' She headed for the stairs, then paused on the first step and half-turned to face him. 'Oh, I nearly forgot: your young cousin was here. Tina. I said you'd gone out and I wasn't expecting you back until teatime. Poor girl. She looked very disappointed to have missed you . . .'

The next day was Saturday and they went to visit Gramps as usual.

Tina and Kirsty were sitting on the floor in the front room, playing one of their video games.

Matt dropped into a space at the end of the sofa and watched their animated characters kicking and hacking their opponents to death. 'What did you want yesterday?' he asked eventually. When there was no sign of a reply, he added, 'When you came to Mrs Eldridge's.'

Kirsty peered at him and Tina said primly, 'I'm afraid I have no idea what it is that you are talking about. You must be mistaken.'

Matt picked up the local paper and scanned through its columns. Let her play her juvenile games if she likes, he decided.

Around mid-morning, his mother came in. She smiled at Matt. 'Want to be useful?' she asked him.

He looked up. Anything to break the monotony, even if it meant spending the afternoon watching washing go round at the laundrette. 'Sure,' he said. 'What is it?'

'You can go out to Crooked Elms with Vince and check on the house,' she said. 'It's been standing empty all this time: you just need to check everything's OK, collect the post – that kind of thing. Vince knows what to do.' She held up a piece of paper. 'There's a list here. A few things Gramps has asked for.'

She glanced at Tina and Kirsty, still engrossed in their game. In a quieter voice, she continued, 'Gramps seemed quite pleased when I suggested you go along – he and Vince don't get on at all well.'

'They hate each other,' said Tina, making them both jump. 'Gramps calls Vince "the Beast".'

The Beast was working on his car in the street outside the house. He was wearing black jeans and a T-shirt, with a pair of wraparound sunglasses pushed back on his head. He looked up after a few seconds, when he became aware that Matt was watching him.

'I . . .' said Matt, hesitating. 'When are you going out to Crooked Elms? Mum wants me to tag along, if that's OK.' He waved the slip of paper. 'She gave me a list.'

Vince rolled his eyes, then spat in the gutter. 'Which do you reckon it is?' he said. 'Either they don't trust me, or they want *you* out of the way. Both, I reckon.'

He sniffed loudly, then ducked under the bonnet once again.

'Soon as I get these plugs back in,' he added.

A few minutes later he straightened, wiping his hands down his jeans. 'All right, then?' he said, dropping the bonnet and heading round to the driver's side. Matt hauled open the nearside door and climbed in.

They drove in silence, until they were dropping down the hill towards the roundabout on the edge of town. 'What's on your list, then?' asked Vince. 'They never give *me* lists.'

'Nothing much,' said Matt. 'Some clothes, a couple of books, their old photo albums.'

Vince snorted. 'I could have got all that for him weeks ago. All he had to do was ask!'

'Maybe it's Mum,' said Matt, although he knew that the list was his grandfather's. 'Maybe it's her idea.'

Vince said nothing as he swung the car around the roundabout. The main road would have taken them on to Colchester; the small road he took would bring them to Crooked Elms in two or three miles.

'Why don't you and Gramps get on?' Matt asked cautiously. In truth, nobody in the family seemed to get on with Vince, but it was Gramps in particular who would have nothing to do with him.

Vince smiled, raising his dark eyebrows. 'He never did like me,' he said. 'Not since I first came into this weird family.'

Matt wondered at his strange choice of phrase, but not for long.

'I'm the outsider,' Vince continued. 'There's no Wareden blood in *me*. See, I was adopted when I was little. Carol and Mike thought they couldn't have children, so they settled for me instead. It often works like that: you can't have children, so you adopt, then suddenly it frees something up and you *can* have kids. Turns out you weren't firing blanks at all, it's just psychological. So they had the ugly sisters and suddenly they wished they'd never bothered with Vince.'

'But . . .' Matt didn't know what he had been going to say, so he shut up. It seemed obvious, now that Vince had explained that he was adopted: he just didn't look like part of this family. Matt's parents had never mentioned it . . . but then they never really talked about this side of the family at all.

'The old boy doesn't trust me,' Vince went on. 'He can't fathom me, and since the business with the old girl . . . He really hates having to live under the same roof. When he was at Crooked Elms he could pretend I'd never happened, but he can't any more.' Then he smiled, adding, 'And he really hates me having *those*.' He pointed at a bunch of keys resting

on the dashboard: presumably the keys to Gramps'
house.

The road climbed up a sudden bank, and through
the high hedgerows Matt saw the first fringe of
Copperas Wood. They must be close to Crooked
Elms, then.

'What do you mean – the "business" with Gran?
What happened?' he asked, watching Vince carefully out of the corner of his eye. 'I know there was
an inquest.'

Vince glanced at him. 'She fell,' he said. 'Gramps
found her at the bottom of the stairs. They had to
have an inquest because they didn't know if she had
had the heart attack and *then* fell, or if she fell and
had the heart attack from the shock.'

They pulled up in the semicircular drive. In silence,
they both looked suspiciously at the house, almost
as if they expected it to do something.

Vince sighed. 'I'm glad I'm not a part of this,' he
said. 'Glad there's none of your freakish blood in
my veins.'

'What do you mean?' Matt asked defensively.

Vince turned to stare at him, dark eyes boring
intensely out of his pale face. He grinned. 'You must
have noticed it,' he said. 'You're not as dumb as the
rest of them. Why do you think Mike'd rather be
down the pub than at home with his own flesh and
blood? Why do you think I hate the lot of them so
much?' After a slight pause, he went on, 'It's in the
blood – the family's blighted.'

'What do you mean?' Matt asked again.

'The Waredens: they all crack up in the end. Gramps has been going loopy for years – if you ask me, I reckon Gran jumped: couldn't bear it any longer. Carol's been on the edge of a nervous breakdown for years, too. And the ugly sisters! Christ, look at the two of them. One of them a control freak, and the other one hardly speaks a word and then keeps having her turns. What a family!'

'In the genes, you mean?'

Vince shrugged. 'Put it this way,' he said. 'If it is, then at least *I'm* in the clear. Me and Mike are the only sane ones there.'

It all sounded a bit extreme to Matt. Sure, he'd noticed how strange Aunt Carol's family was – you couldn't miss it. But if it was in the blood, then why had he and his mother missed out? Assuming they had, of course . . .

He didn't want to leave the car, he realized. He wanted to stay in his seat – let Vince go and check everything and find the things on the list while he just sat here.

He had felt like this before, after the funeral, when they had returned from the crematorium. He could just stay here, perhaps. He could come up with some excuse that Vince would swallow.

'You feel it too, do you?' Vince said softly, making Matt jump.

He did, but he didn't know what *it* was.

'Some places are like that,' Vince continued.

'Some people, too: they can sense a lot more about a place than anyone can just through sight or smell. They can sense its history, its power.'

Neither of them moved.

'I know about these things,' said Vince. 'I've studied them. Some places are special, they have an energy all their own. This place is special, Matt. There are dark powers at work here.'

Suddenly the tension became too much for Matt and he snorted with laughter. Stopping himself immediately, he looked at Vince. His cousin had gone even paler than before, with sudden dark lines etched across his forehead.

'It's real!' he hissed. 'You wouldn't laugh if you knew about these things like I do.'

'Sorry,' gasped Matt. 'I . . .'

'I *know* about these things,' said Vince through gritted teeth. 'I'm genuine, man. I'm *real*.'

Vince reached into the glove compartment and removed something. There was a click and suddenly a blade appeared to leap up from his clenched fist: he had a flick knife.

Matt sank back in his seat.

'I'm real, man. Don't ever doubt me.'

Vince raised the knife, then slowly pressed its blade against his forearm and dragged it back towards his elbow. A band of scarlet appeared across his pale skin, and all the time his eyes never left Matt's face.

He moved his hand and dragged the blade across his arm again, leaving a second bleeding line.

He raised the knife again and Matt said, 'OK, OK! I believe you – OK?'

Vince wiped the blade on his jeans, retracted it, and tossed the knife on to the back seat. 'Don't ever doubt me, you hear?' he said. 'Don't ever doubt me.'

Matt took the keys and left Vince sitting in the car, hands gripping the steering wheel, eyes locked straight ahead.

He had never been so scared in all his life.

For all he had said about the others, Vince was the maddest member of that family, Wareden blood or not.

Matt opened the front door, pushing a small pile of mail to one side. He squatted to gather up the letters.

The stairs were immediately in front of him and he realized he was crouching in the spot where his grandmother must have drawn her final breath. The stairs were steep: an old woman could easily lose her footing and fall, he supposed.

The place was hot and airless. There was a huge polished ammonite by the front door. He used it to prop the door open.

He walked along the corridor, trying to stay calm.

It was only a house.

A big, empty house.

He pushed at the kitchen door, his heart pounding. South facing, the room was flooded with bright sunlight. He squinted around. There was nothing out of place.

He turned, walked along the corridor and opened the next door, remembering that this was the living-room, where they had all gathered after the funeral. There were two fireplaces: one full of old ashes, the other long disused, housing an arrangement of dried flowers and grasses.

He remembered the day of the funeral quite clearly now. He remembered the sherry sticking to the lining of his throat, the intense heat of the fire.

He shook his head vigorously, as a sudden wave of nausea threatened to engulf him.

The next room was the library, where Gran had been laid out before the funeral. It was cooler here, the atmosphere calmer.

Atmosphere ... He was letting himself get spooked by Vince's irrational behaviour.

He went to each room in turn, until he had been through the entire house, opening every door until he was sure everything was OK: no break-ins, no leaking pipes, nothing out of place.

He checked his list.

He was already upstairs, so he went to the main bedroom first of all. *Large chest, third drawer down*, the list told him. He found the shirts, each neatly folded. He placed two in the bag he had brought and eased the drawer shut.

Downstairs in the library, he went straight to the cupboard that held the photo albums. These were for his mother, he knew. *As many as you can manage*, she had scrawled on the list. The cupboard was full of them: from modern flip-over ones to heavy, old, board-covered albums with faded grey pictures pasted on to pages that were separated by thin, protective interleaves.

He took four of the older-looking volumes and stacked them with the clothes bag by the front door. As he did so, he looked out to the car. Vince was still sitting in the driver's seat, shades pushed down to hide his eyes. He was puffing casually on a cigarette.

The last items on the list were the two books: first editions, they were in a box in the basement. Apparently Gramps had packed them up, ready to be sent off for sale, just before Gran died.

Matt opened the basement door, savouring the cool, damp air that drifted out. He stepped inside, found the light switch and looked around. A flight of concrete stairs dropped away in front of him. The walls on either side were of red brick, worn smooth by generations of use.

He gripped the hand-rail and headed down.

The basement opened out on his left, a low-ceilinged chamber strewn with boxes and bags and all kinds of junk. It seemed to go on forever: he couldn't see the farthest wall – the light just faded to blackness. There was a sense of enormous space here, of great age, too. His heart was racing, he realized. He made himself calm down.

Straight ahead of you. A brown Post Office parcel box.

He saw it immediately, relieved that he wouldn't have to go too far into the basement and trawl through all this debris. He stepped forward, felt suddenly dizzy and lurched towards the wall.

What was happening?

The bricks were cool against his cheek and suddenly he remembered his recurring dream: the high brick walls, the concrete floor. A dark presence, following him.

He pushed himself away from the wall and tried to approach the box. It felt as if his feet were stuck to the ground, as if he were wearing lead shoes.

The box. He had to get the box.

His heart was drumming in his ears, his breathing ragged, painful.

The heat! Why had he thought it so cool? The place was like a furnace.

At any moment his legs would crumple and he would collapse to the ground. But he knew that if he did he would never get up.

He forced himself to turn, finding it easier to drag his feet back towards the stairs.

He reached the first step and slumped forward. In this position, he hauled himself up, one step at a time.

He had only made it about half way when he blacked out.

Hands on his arms, turning him, pinching at his cheeks, slapping him. A white face like a skull looming over him, dark eyes.

'Do you believe me now, then?'

It was Vince.

Matt shook the hands free, then rose to a sitting position. He was in the hallway. The box of books was at his side, even though he couldn't remember picking them up.

'Found you on the stairs, didn't I?' said Vince. 'Looks like you had a turn, just like Kirsty.' He looked around. 'It's this place; it gets to her, too.' He was grinning now, chuckling to himself. 'Looks like you've got it too, then: the madness of the Waredens. Looks like you're just as bad as the rest of them . . .'

5

GRAMPS

'The books?' Gramps asked, as soon as Matt entered Aunt Carol's front room. 'Did you manage to get the books?'

Matt nodded. 'The box is in the car,' he said. 'I'll bring them in, if you like.'

Gramps' eyes narrowed and he pursed his lips. He said nothing and Matt felt he had to fill the silence.

'I got the rest of your things, too,' he continued. 'The house was fine – a bit airless, that's all.'

Gramps was still watching him. 'That place has been in the family for years,' he said. 'I was born there. I bet you didn't know that, did you?'

Matt shook his head, although Gramps had told him the same thing only two days earlier.

'Lunch?' Carol said brightly, sweeping past Matt into the room.

That afternoon, Matt just had to get away, and as he left the house he felt a great weight lifting.

Throughout lunch, Vince had sat there, watching him. He made no attempt to hide the parallel cuts on his arm and nobody commented on them. And all the time Matt was aware of his watching eyes, his smug grin.

Now, he crossed Bay Road by the memorial and headed down one of the zigzag paths to the Promenade.

It was a Saturday in August and the place was seething with people. It felt good to be among so many ordinary – *normal* – people. Overweight parents watching their naked, overweight toddlers paddling on the beach. Gangs of young children chasing each other along the Prom and up and down the steep, grassy slope locals called 'the cliff'. Old folks calling helplessly after dogs that, according to the numerous notices, should be on leads at all times, with a £50 penalty. Teenagers down on the beach in bathing costumes and long shorts, smoking cigarettes and drinking lager from cans.

Matt thought about his friends in Norwich. They all seemed so far away. Why would nobody tell him why they had to stay down here for so long, why his life was being messed about in this way? Nobody had consulted him about any of it; he had simply been told he was coming to Bathside with his mother.

She hadn't told him it would be for so long. She hadn't told him anything, so now he could only guess why she was avoiding questions about when they would go home and why his father never answered his calls.

He'd confronted her last night and demanded to

know how long they would be staying. 'I'm sorry, Matt,' she had told him. 'It's not easy. Gramps . . . I can't just *leave*. Anyway, it's the summer and we're by the sea: why not treat it like a holiday?'

He found a space on the grassy 'cliff' and lay back. It wasn't as hot as it had been a few days ago, but the hazy sun felt good as its rays soaked into his weary body. Closing his eyes, with the smell of the sea and the sounds of the people all round him, he tried to imagine that he really *was* on holiday.

Instead, he remembered Vince's mad, staring eyes and the look – almost of pleasure, he realized – on his face as he had dragged that blade up his arm. He remembered the tension in his cousin's voice as he had said, 'I'm real, man. Don't ever doubt me.'

No wonder he had overreacted. That's what it was, he was sure. Sitting in the car on the way back to Bathside, he had thought through his experience at the house – in the basement. It was delayed shock, he was sure. He remembered how scared he had been by Vince's actions, how he had forced it out of his mind and had gone into the house. He had moved from room to room like some kind of robot: checking that everything was OK, finding the items on his list.

And then in the basement . . . Had he stumbled, perhaps? Was that what had broken through his barriers and let the panic come rushing out? It was all a perfectly natural response to Vince's warped display of bravado.

He smiled grimly. Either that, or he was cracking up, just like the rest of his family . . .

He knew something was wrong as soon as he entered the Bed-and-Breakfast in Bagshaw Terrace. There was something about it, although he didn't know quite what it was.

Mrs Eldridge was working in the kitchen, singing a hymn in an exaggerated, semi-operatic voice. Her little daughter Lauren was in the front room, watching one of her videos as usual. So why was he suddenly so edgy? What was it that his body had detected that his mind couldn't quite put into words?

He noticed the smell as he started up the second flight of stairs. A briny, pungent tang. Like old, rotting seaweed.

Automatically, he looked down at his feet. He had been on the beach earlier, but there was nothing attached to his shoes that could have brought this smell into the house with him.

The smell had become quite foul by the time he reached the top landing.

His mother's door was open and as soon as she heard him she stepped into view. Her face was pale, and he could see from the redness round her eyes that she had been crying.

'What . . . what is it?' he asked.

She pushed a wisp of hair out of her eyes. 'Matthew,' she said in a steady, controlled tone. 'I know it's been hard for you, but *really* . . .'

'What?'

'I *know* you must be bored out of your mind, but this is really too much.'

'*What* is?' He stepped into the room, and the smell was so strong now that he nearly retched.

'This . . . this macabre collecting of yours: I didn't say anything the first time, but it's going to have to stop, do you hear me? It's disgusting, Matt: these things are full of germs and God knows what else, and it stinks to high heaven! I really don't know what's got into that mind of yours. I really don't understand what's got into you.'

He still stared at her blankly, so she stopped talking and merely pointed at a carrier bag on one of the twin beds in his room. 'Just get rid of it,' she said. 'Just get rid of that thing and we'll forget all about it, OK?'

She was clearly making a tremendous effort to be understanding and reasonable, and Matt still had no idea what she was talking about.

He went over to the bed. The stench was quite unbearable. Tentatively, he reached out for the bag and pulled it open.

Feathers. White or grey, matted a foul, dark red. A slim red beak, half open, a fly crawling about in the empty gape.

It was a seagull, dead for several days, judging by the state of it, and the smell.

Matt looked at his mother. How could she accuse him of this?

She was staring at him, still trying to be understanding. 'Where did it come from?' he asked.

'It was there when I came in, a few minutes ago,' she said. 'You really should know not to do something like this.'

'But . . .' There was no point in arguing. She was never going to believe him: she'd already made up her mind that he was guilty. The more he protested his innocence, the more *understanding* she would try to be.

He gathered up the bag, overcoming a wave of nausea as he did so, and headed out of the room.

He hurried out through the conservatory and into the back alley, all the time aware of the thing in the bag. He turned left in the alley, and moments later he was standing on the pavement of Bay Road, wondering what he was going to do.

It had to be Tina, he knew: trying to drive them away from Bathside. Maybe it would work, he mused. Maybe his mother would be so worried about his mental health that she would want to get back to Norwich as soon as possible.

An old man, passing along the pavement, peered at Matt and wrinkled his nose up in disgust. Matt had grown used to the foul smell by now, forgetting how strong it was.

He crossed the road and walked along the top of the grassy cliff.

After a short distance, he came to a bin and, relieved, he dumped the plastic bag inside.

Back at the Bed-and-Breakfast, his mother was waiting.

'Guess what?' she said, more relaxed now, trying to smile.

He raised his eyebrows, still angry at her false accusation.

'Dinner with your aunt and uncle for a change.' She studied his expression, then added, 'I knew you'd be pleased.'

A familiar scene: Gramps slumped silently in what had become his armchair, the girls sitting cross-legged on the floor, slaughtering animated foes on the TV, Matt sitting at one end of the sofa and staring out of the window.

For a while he watched the back of Tina's head, hating every movement. Eventually, she turned and smiled at him. 'Has Aunty Jill had enough yet?' she asked. 'Are you going back to Norwich?'

Matt stood up and walked out of the room. How do you handle someone like Tina? What could he possibly do that would get through to her? He remembered Vince saying that it was like living in an asylum. Matt knew now exactly what he meant.

That evening, after they had eaten, Gramps said, 'Air.' He waved a hand in front of his face. 'I need air.'

Carol rose to her feet instantly. She put a hand on her father's arm and said, 'I'll take you for your walk.' Every evening someone would take Gramps for a slow walk around the garden.

But tonight he shook off her hand. He looked at Matt and said, 'Matthew, my boy. Join me?'

Surprised, Matt nodded.

It was quite cool outside now, a breeze coming in off the sea. As Matt waited on the patio, holding the door for his grandfather, a pair of small bats flitted about the eaves of the house.

'The moths come for the honeysuckle, the bats come for the moths,' said Gramps. He waved in the direction of the honeysuckle that scrambled over a trellis on the back wall. Matt was surprised that his eyes were still sharp enough to see in this murky twilight.

They walked slowly along the patio, Matt unsure whether he should offer his grandfather support or not. He chose not to, and just walked close beside him.

'Like Bathside, do you?' Gramps asked. 'The sea? The beach?'

'It's OK,' said Matt.

Gramps nodded. 'Your mother doesn't,' he said. 'She's not happy, although she tries to hide it. Never liked this place. Couldn't wait to get away from here when she was a girl – took the first chance she could. Never liked to come back, even to visit. We make her uneasy.' He smiled sadly at this.

Matt was taken by surprise. He had been sure it was his father who had been the reason for their infrequent visits, not his mother.

At the bottom of the garden there was a stone bench, its surface weather-stained and mottled with lichen. Gramps lowered himself on to the seat and, after a moment's hesitation, Matt joined him.

'You found my books all right, then.'

Matt was surprised to remember that it was only this morning that he had gone out to Crooked Elms with Vince. It all seemed so long ago, somehow. He nodded. 'In the basement,' he said. 'Just like it said on the list.'

His grandfather was peering at him, his pale blue eyes picking up the lights from the house so that they shone eerily in the dusk shadows. 'You . . . you didn't have any trouble?'

Matt started to shake his head, then stopped, unsure. 'I fell over,' he said. 'Hit my head, I think. But it's OK – I didn't break anything.'

'You came to stay with us when you were five months old,' Gramps said abruptly. 'Screamed the place down for most of two days. I said then that you were a sensitive one. Dizzy, were you? Did you feel the heat? Did you see anything?'

Matt shuddered, unnerved by his grandfather's words. He remembered Vince talking about dark powers, special places, the family madness. 'I just fell,' he said. 'Tripped over something, I suppose. I blacked out for a short time and then Vince came and helped me.'

Gramps gasped. 'Vincent?' he hissed. 'He was there with you?'

'He drove me there,' Matt said patiently. 'He has the keys.'

'What happened? What did he do?'

Matt glanced towards the house, worried by his grandfather's sudden agitation. 'Nothing,' he said, remembering Vince's mad stare as he had so carefully slashed his own arm. 'He sat in the car most of the time, then he helped me with the box. That's all.'

Gramps gripped his arm tightly. 'You should be careful of that one,' he said. 'He doesn't know how dangerous he is, dabbling in things he doesn't understand. He's not a Wareden, you know – not really one of us at all. Doesn't have the Wareden insight . . . doesn't have the sensitivity . . . doesn't appreciate the family way. Do you understand me, boy? Do you?'

Gramps was panting rapidly, hyperventilating.

Matt stood. 'I'll just go and get Mum,' he said, backing away.

Gramps half stood, then slumped back on to the bench. 'No,' he said. 'No, Matthew! I need to talk to you. I need to warn you, don't you understand?'

'Calm down, Gramps,' said Matt, scared by the sudden intensity of the old man. 'Later, OK? We'll talk later. You just need to calm down now, OK?'

But his grandfather pushed himself up again, and this time he managed to stand. 'No,' he said. 'Now . . . now's the time to . . .'

Matt turned and ran.

A moment later, he burst in through the back door. Carol took one look at him and rushed out, past him, into the growing darkness.

His mother was slower to react. She stared at him. 'What is it?' she asked.

'Gramps,' said Matt. 'He started ranting, started to shout . . . to get over-excited.' He thought then of Vince's words. 'I think he's gone mad,' he said. 'I think he's finally flipped.'

Gramps had fallen over on to the lawn.

When Matt saw Carol crouching by him, he feared the very worst.

Then he heard his grandfather's voice, mumbling away, the words completely unintelligible by now.

Carol turned the old man on to his side, and when Matt's mother joined her the two of them were able to raise Gramps to a sitting position.

Matt stood back, wishing he could disappear completely in the shadows, as they helped Gramps back into the house. Uncle Mike was standing in the doorway, watching it all with a drunken smile on his face.

As they took Gramps to his room, Mike burped softly into the back of his hand.

'Good one,' he said, turning to Matt. 'Got him well worked up, didn't you? How did you do it? Maybe I'll have a go myself, next time.'

6

EVERYTHING
CHANGES

Matt spent most of the next morning in Mrs Eldridge's conservatory, reading another second-rate thriller. They went to Aunt Carol's for lunch, as usual.

Gramps had been in bed all morning. 'It's OK,' said Carol sympathetically, when Matt clearly looked concerned. 'He's just a bit low. A bit tired . . . You know how it is.'

Matt nodded. He remembered Gramps' rantings from the previous evening. Gramps had wanted to tell him something. 'Can I go up and see him?' he asked now.

Carol shook her head emphatically. 'Like I said: he's tired. Let him rest today. See how he is in the morning. All right, darling?'

He shrugged. It wasn't all that important, he supposed.

That afternoon his mother was called away to the telephone.

Matt was sitting outside, reading. The first he knew about it was when Tina found him.

She was smiling. He looked up at her, resenting her intrusion on his peace. He never liked it when the girl smiled, it nearly always meant something bad.

'What is it?' he grunted, when she refused to vanish in a puff of smoke as he had been hoping.

'Aunty Jill had a telephone call,' she said.

'So?'

'I think it was probably bad news. She put the phone down so hard I was sure she was going to break it. She really should know better.'

She stood there, still smiling, still refusing to vanish. Matt returned his eyes to the pages of his book, but he couldn't concentrate while his ghoulish cousin was standing over him like that.

'She was crying,' Tina said eventually. 'Then she rushed out of the room. I didn't know Aunty Jill was so unstable.'

'Why are you telling me all this?' Matt asked, although he had a pretty good idea of the answer.

Her smile grew even broader. 'Because Mum brought me up to be helpful and considerate,' she said. 'And because I hate you.'

He went into the house.

Carol was in the kitchen, rolling pastry. The pastry formed a near-perfect circle, as if it didn't dare go against his aunt's wishes.

'Where's Mum?'

She looked up, then looked away again quickly. That wasn't like her at all.

'She had to go back to Bagshaw Terrace,' she said. 'She'll be back soon – perhaps you should wait.' She added this as Matt turned instantly and headed along the hall to the front door. He ignored her and went outside.

He found his mother in her room, struggling to stuff their belongings into the bags they had brought with them on the train from Norwich. For a moment his heart leapt as he thought Tina was going to get her wish and they were finally going home. Then he saw the look on his mother's face, and he knew immediately it was far worse than that.

'I'm sorry, Matt,' she said, as he stopped in the doorway. She forced the zip closed on her bag and rubbed vigorously at her eyes. 'We can't live here with Mrs Eldridge any more. We're going to have to stay with Aunt Carol for a few days, until we sort something else out.'

For an insane moment, Matt wondered what Tina had done now to get them kicked out of their lodgings. Then he dismissed the thought.

'What is it?' he demanded. 'What's going on?'

'It's your father,' she said hesitantly, refusing to meet his demanding stare. 'He hasn't been paying. Mrs Eldridge won't put us up without being paid any money.'

'Call him, then. Ask him for the money.' He didn't see the problem. He *refused* to see the problem.

She just looked at him. Then she reached up and swept the hair back out of her eyes. 'No, Matt. It's no good. He says he won't pay anything until he's made to.'

It started to sink in, at last: the meaning of her words. Confirming his darkest fears.

His parents had split up.

The only thing that broke through his initial sense of shock was the look of dismay on Tina's face when Matt and his mother turned up at Aunt Carol's house with their bags. Her mouth fell open, her eyes bulged as if they would pop out of their sockets at any moment, and she stared – how she stared!

'Come on,' said Carol, taking the bag from his mother and turning towards the stairs. 'We'll put your things in your room. It's all ready for you. OK?'

Matt followed the two of them up the stairs. He remembered that this had been a guest-house at one time, so there were plenty of rooms.

They went up to the second floor, just as if they were still at Mrs Eldridge's. 'You can have this one,' Carol said brightly to her sister, stepping through a doorway. She looked back at Matt and added, 'The door behind you, Matthew. It's small, I'm afraid, but I'm sure it will do for now.'

He turned and pushed at the white, panelled door before him. It opened on to a square box-room, clearly used for storage: it was full of packing cases, cardboard boxes, old suitcases and bags, all stuffed full of things. Piled on top of the boxes and bags were several years' worth of assorted junk: ornamental lamps, a full-length mirror, an old kettle, shoes, books, string-bound bundles of magazines, stacked dining chairs, bundled sleeping-bags, a guitar without strings, what looked like a deflated paddling pool, a box marked XMAS DECS.

He took it all in. This was it, he realized. Everything had changed.

The junk had been cleared away from one side of the room so that a camp bed could be fitted in – the room was barely long enough to allow the bed to be fully opened out. Matt dumped his bag on the floor and leant over to prod suspiciously at the bed. He went across to the small window. The room was at the back of the house, and he found he was looking out over the garden and across to the next row of terraced houses.

He remembered sitting out there on the stone bench only the previous evening, listening to Gramps getting steadily more worked up until he had his fit, or whatever it was.

Carol's voice drifted across the landing, like the incessant twittering of a caged bird. He walked across – four paces – and shut the door softly. He sat on the bed and unzipped his bag. He found his books and his signed photograph of Michael Owen and arranged them along the mantelpiece above a boarded-up fireplace, and then he lay back on his bed, folded his hands behind his head and stared at the ceiling.

So this is it.

This made his moods of the last few days seem so petty: sulking because the first couple of weeks of his summer holidays had been messed up. Everything was different now, all the certainty had been removed from his life. All the things he had taken for granted – home, friends, school, the relentless course of the next few years as he approached adulthood – had been cast into doubt.

And it *hurt*. There was a tight knot of pain buried deep in his chest, in his gut. He thought he might be sick, but he fought the feeling. He wasn't going to let them do that to him. No tears, either.

Just the pain.

Had they actually *moved* to Bathside, he wondered. Was this to be his home, his future? Was he to have no say in it?

He tried to stop thinking, tried to ignore how much it hurt.

She came in to see him some time later. He didn't know how long he had been lying there alone, staring at the ceiling, running the same thoughts round and round in his head as if somehow that would change anything.

She tapped at the door first. Then, when he said nothing, she pushed it open tentatively. 'Hi,' she said, an uneasy smile breaking briefly across her face. 'Comfortable?'

Sure, he was comfortable. Never better. He said nothing.

She looked around. Matt guessed she wanted to sit down so that she wasn't looming over him like that, but there were no usable chairs and the bed was too flimsy for the two of them. She leant on the wall, then straightened up, then finally settled for squatting on her haunches with one shoulder against the wall. Getting down to the same level – as if she was talking to a toddler, or a dog, Matt thought.

'You won't have to put up with all this for long, love,' she told him. 'I'll sort something out.'

'*What* will you sort out?' Matt demanded. 'Are we going back to Norwich? What about Dad?'

She brushed at her hair with a clawed hand. 'I don't know,' she said. Then she shook her head decisively. 'No,' she corrected herself. 'I do know. I'm not going back. I told Carol I'm going to find work down here, then find somewhere to live.'

'And me?' As soon as he heard his own words, it sounded so selfish. He wasn't the only one whose life had been ripped apart. 'What about me?'

'We thought it best you stay here, for the time being. Your father is travelling a lot over the next couple of weeks.' She swept her hair back again with a sudden, jerky movement that made Matt jump. Then she went on, 'You're old enough to decide what's best for you. You need to do what you think is right. But, Matt, I love you . . . I want you to stay with me.'

'You knew all along, didn't you?' said Matt. 'When we came down here – you knew you were leaving Dad. You knew you were breaking up.'

His words hurt her, he could see, and he felt a small thrill of satisfaction.

She shook her head. 'I didn't know that that was it,' she said in an unsteady voice. 'But it has been on the cards for a long time, Matt – you must have been aware. Suddenly, coming here . . . it made me think . . . And then it just happened.' She gathered herself, then continued, 'I spoke to your father on the phone this afternoon and it was only then that I actually realized we'd split up. It just happened, Matt. It wasn't planned, it wasn't deliberate. It just happened.'

He rolled over on to his side so that his back was to his mother. He had stared at the ceiling for long enough. Now he would stare at the wall.

That night, everything changed again.

Matt had never endured a more strained evening. He refused to acknowledge his mother's presence, even though she was constantly on the verge of tears. Uncle Mike glowered at everyone, making it quite clear that this arrangement wasn't going to last for long if *he* had anything to do with it.

Matt couldn't bear it. He couldn't get his mind straight. He pushed his chair away from the table, aware that all eyes were turning towards him.

Away from the dining room, he felt some of the pressure lifting. He decided to go up for his book, although he knew he wouldn't be able to concentrate.

On the first floor, he hesitated.

Gramps had been up here all day. His door was open now and Matt could see him, sitting in an armchair in his pyjamas and dressing gown, poring over one of his old photograph albums.

Matt was surprised to see his grandfather looking so calm. So normal. He approached the door and then, when Gramps looked up, he went in and sat on the edge of the bed. The room smelt of scotch – a near-empty bottle stood on top of a chest of drawers near by.

No wonder Gramps seemed so placid, Matt thought. He'd been up here all day, drinking himself senseless.

'You wanted to tell me something,' said Matt. 'Yesterday, when we were in the garden. There was something you wanted to say.'

Gramps looked puzzled for a moment, his pale blue eyes glazing over. 'Oh,' he said. Then he seemed to understand. 'Oh yes,' he said. He waved a hand dismissively. 'Later,' he continued. 'You'll understand it all later.' He smiled. He didn't seem able to talk in more than a short sentence at a time this evening. 'I've written it all down.' He waved at a pile of letters on a chair at the foot of the bed. 'Can't seem to concentrate. It's better written down. Says everything.' He gestured at the letters again. 'One of them's for you, boy. Go on: take it. You can read it later.'

Matt leant across and picked up the stack of letters. Each was in its own envelope, with a name in small, neat handwriting. *Carol*, *Jill*, *Kirsty*, *Tina*. And there, at the bottom of the pile, *Matthew*.

He took the letter and replaced the others on the

chair. Gramps must have been working all day at these letters. Whatever he had to say, it must be important.

'Ever wanted to do something you're almost too scared to do?' Gramps asked, a strange intensity in his eyes. 'But it's your only real choice?'

Matt didn't understand. He watched his grandfather cautiously, saw that his eyes were glazed again. Too much drink, he thought.

And then he *did* start to understand: Gramps' strange calmness, his inability to string together more than a few words at a time. The letters – there was something horribly final about those letters.

Matt looked across at the chest of drawers ... the nearly empty scotch bottle. There was something else lying there, something he had seen earlier, although he had not fully appreciated its significance.

It was a small bottle with a printed label. The kind that prescriptions come in.

It was lying on its side with its cap off, and it was empty. His grandfather's words suddenly made sense: *Ever wanted to do something you're almost too scared to do? But it's your only real choice?*

Gramps had taken an overdose.

Matt's eyes moved from the empty pill-bottle to Gramps, then back again.

Then he leapt to his feet and dashed across the room to the landing. He had to get help, if he wasn't already too late.

'Mum!' he called, the first time he had tried to speak to her since this afternoon. 'Mum! It's Gramps! He needs help!'

7

WAITING

Aunt Carol appeared at the foot of the stairs, her face pale – clearly alerted by the tone of Matt's voice.

'What . . .?' She only had to look at him to be galvanized into action. She rushed up the stairs, her footsteps thudding in rapid, staccato succession, like a boxer striking a punchbag.

'He's taken some pills,' Matt said, as she hurried past him across the landing. 'He's taken some pills.'

Downstairs, his mother had appeared, followed by Uncle Mike. Matt looked at them, then at Carol's retreating back. He felt helpless. He felt *responsible*.

He hurried back into Gramps' room, as more steps sounded on the stairs.

Carol was by her father's side. 'Dad? Dad? What have you done? *Dad?*'

Gramps was staring blankly across the room, a half-smile on his face. Slowly, he turned his eyes on his daughter. 'Carol?' he said, in little more than a whisper. 'Don't worry, Carol. I'll look for your mother, I will.'

She looked up at Matt. 'What's he taken?' she asked.

Matt pointed to the chest of drawers, the evidence of Gramps' actions.

'I came up a few minutes ago,' he said. He knew it was important to get the facts straight. He struggled to think. 'He seemed OK – very calm. He's been drinking and he must have taken those pills.'

His mother appeared in the doorway, followed by Mike, Vince and the girls.

'The bottle's empty,' Matt added. 'He's been writing letters, too.'

Carol took the pills from the chest and studied the label, then she glanced down at the letters on the chair at the foot of the bed. 'Call an ambulance,' she said. She looked up and saw everyone in the doorway. 'Jill, call an ambulance,' she said. 'And everyone else can just get downstairs! Mike – what are you thinking of, bringing the girls up here?'

Mike looked around, as if surprised that he had been followed. He put his arms round his daughters and shepherded them away. Matt's mother was already downstairs, tapping out 999 on the telephone.

As Matt backed out of the room, he saw Carol sweep up the letters and then return to crouch before her father, hanging desperately on to his hand, as if that would make any difference.

Matt joined Vince on the landing.

Vince shook his head. 'The old goat certainly

knows how to liven things up, doesn't he?' his cousin said in a conversational tone. He turned to make his way down the stairs. 'Fancy a drink?' he asked Matt. 'There's some cans in the fridge.'

They retreated to the living room, where Kirsty was crying into her sister's shoulder. Over Kirsty's head, Tina glowered accusingly at Matt, as if it was all *his* fault.

Matt's mother appeared a few seconds later. 'They're on their way,' she said. She went over to Kirsty and Tina and gave them a little hug. 'He'll be OK,' she said.

Tina glared at her, stiffening at her touch.

Just then, Vince came into the room, carrying a six-pack of Heineken. He broke one away from its plastic binding and tossed it to Matt.

Matt's mother looked at the beer but said nothing. Vince held out the remaining cans to her, but she shook her head. Instead, he ripped another one away and handed it to Mike, then he sat on the sofa with what was left.

Matt opened his can and took a long, cool drink, as his mother left the room and hurried back upstairs.

His hand started to shake and he put the can down on the coffee table.

He couldn't get his grandfather's glazed, contented look out of his head. Why had he taken so long to realize what had happened? He had seen the bottle and the empty pill-jar as soon as he entered the room, yet it had taken him several long minutes to understand what they meant.

He had another drink, and forced his hands to stop shaking. Delayed reaction, he supposed. Shock. It's not every day you talk to somebody who's in the process of killing himself.

The ambulance came, and the paramedics carried Gramps downstairs, strapped on a stretcher. Carol and her sister went with him to the hospital, leaving Matt and the others to wait at home.

A short time after the ambulance had gone, Mike tried to persuade Tina and Kirsty that they should go to bed. They refused to go. 'We're hardly going to be able to sleep, are we?' said Tina, quite sensibly. 'And it's not even Kirsty's bedtime yet.' They settled down in a corner of the living room to look at a large, colourful book about coral reefs, Tina explaining everything to her sister in great detail.

She was showing off, Matt realized: this was a chance for her to show how grown-up she could be, reassuring and distracting her young sister.

Matt sat on the sofa, working his way steadily down the can of lager and leafing through a mail order catalogue. After about half an hour, he had chosen the best video, hi-fi, TV and computer, and he had just moved on to the tents when the telephone rang.

Mike grabbed the receiver, snapped, 'Yes,' and then listened for several seconds. Everyone watched him as he took the call, looking for any sign that would tell them what was happening.

As soon as he put the phone down, Kirsty said, 'What's happened, Dad? Where have they taken Gramps?'

Mike gathered his younger daughter on to his lap. 'They've taken him to the General Hospital,' he said. 'The doctors are trying to make him better now.' He looked over Kirsty's head at the others and added, 'Mum'll call again when she knows any more.'

So they sat and waited as before, playing video games, reading, watching TV. Occasionally, one of them tried to make conversation – the weather, the new road they wanted to build to the south-west of Bathside, Vince's prospects for finding something better than the casual labouring work he had at the moment. 'What are you going to do now?' Vince asked Matt, changing the subject swiftly away from the last of these topics.

'I don't know,' said Matt. 'Mum's going to find work, and somewhere to live. I might stay with her or I might go back to Norwich to stay with Dad. I don't know.'

Turning to her sister, Tina said, 'Matthew was saying only the other day how much he liked living in Norwich. Wouldn't it be nice if he could live with Uncle Nigel?' Kirsty looked from her sister to Matt and back and smiled uncertainly.

Then, more quietly, Tina added, 'Uncle Nigel and Aunty Jill are going to get a *divorce*. They don't like each other any more.'

'Washing up,' Mike butted in, realizing too late what his daughter was saying. 'Come on, girls. I'll wash and you two can dry. OK?'

At that moment the telephone rang again. Matt looked at his watch with a start: it was well past eleven o'clock. They had been waiting for over two hours since Carol's first call from the hospital.

Mike answered and listened to what his wife had to say. 'OK,' he said. 'See you soon.' And, 'Yes, they'll be in bed.'

He put the receiver down and Matt saw that his uncle was looking relieved. 'He's OK,' he said. 'They got to him in time. He's going to survive.'

PART THREE
ALTERNITY

8

THE WAREDENS OF CROOKED ELMS

About fifteen minutes later, Matt heard the sound of a car pulling up at the front of the house. Mike was still upstairs with Tina and Kirsty, making sure they were settled for the night, and Vince had gone off to his room, losing interest as soon as Carol had called to say things were OK.

Matt looked out of the window and saw his aunt passing some money through the window of a taxi. He went to open the door. Carol and his mother looked terrible: pale-faced, heavy shadows under their tired-looking eyes.

'Thanks,' said Carol, brushing past him. Then she paused and turned back towards him. 'You were just in time,' she said. 'If you hadn't looked in on him when you did . . .'

Matt didn't know what to say. All evening, his thoughts had kept returning to what had happened. In particular, he kept asking himself, What's Gramps going to think when they've pumped the medicine out of his stomach? Will *he* be grateful? Will *he* praise Matt for being 'just in time'?

His mother took him by surprise and hugged him

as he stood back to let her in. He stood awkwardly until she let go. He still hadn't got things straight in his mind, but he was still angry with her for trying to keep him in the dark – she had admitted what was happening only when there had been no alternative. He wasn't going to forget that in a hurry.

A short time later, he shut the box-room door behind him and leant with his back against it. He was shaking again, still in reaction to the events of the evening – the shock, the fear, the anger.

He stripped and pulled on some pyjama trousers. Then he turned off the light and slipped under the striped cotton sheets, the camp bed's springs groaning beneath him.

He lay for some time with his hands behind his head.

He didn't want to sleep. He wasn't even remotely tired.

He remembered the letter. The suicide note. Was it right to read it, now that Gramps' suicide had been prevented?

He sighed. He knew that, no matter how much he reasoned with himself, his curiosity was certain to win in the end.

He got up again, turned on the light and found the letter in one of the back pockets of his jeans. He climbed back into bed and slid a finger along under the flap.

My dear Matthew,

I will be dead when you read this. Please do not blame me for taking this option: it is not without some deliberation that I decided to end things now. I have gone to the same place as your grandmother, wherever that might be. Life has not been endurable since she was killed.

Matt paused at this point, puzzled by his grandfather's choice of words: 'since she was killed', not 'since she died' or 'since she passed away'. What had happened on that day in the house at Crooked Elms, he wondered.

He returned to the letter:

However, I am not writing to justify my own cowardly actions. This is the last letter I will write; I have already made my excuses in my letters to Carol and Jill.

I am writing to you, especially, Matt. The others are more familiar with the ways of our strange family, but you have grown up apart: what you are experiencing, and what you are to learn, will transform your life. I think you are mature enough to cope. Indeed, I hope that you are, for you must learn either properly now or by accident at some later date.

To the point, I hear you demanding, quite rightly! To the point.

You are gifted, Matt, just as many in our family

have been gifted over the years. But with that gift comes a heavy responsibility, one that I have struggled to bear for my own 88 years.

I will explain the responsibility, and the dangers, but first I must explain the gift.

There is a peculiar and special talent that runs through our family, inherited by roughly half of each generation: Kirsty and you have it, but not, I think, Tina – much to her chagrin! Neither Carol nor Jill have shown any indication of the gift, either.

At this point, Vince's words about the family madness, the special sensitivity, came rushing back: the family curse that only Vince and Mike, not being direct descendants in the Wareden line, could be sure of avoiding.

Have you ever felt the urge to do something you shouldn't? Something you're too frightened even to think about? Everybody has these impulses, but most of us are able to keep them under control. Battling inside our heads is a whole set of alternative selves – the people we might have been, if only things had turned out differently.

But it's not as simple as that. The realm of the mind is every bit as real as what we call reality. Carl Jung was close to the mark when he talked of the collective unconscious. That shared mental realm is another world: a kind of hell, if you will.

Its darker reaches surface in our dreams, and in the minds of the unstable.

Rare individuals among us are especially sensitive to this other realm, this Alternity. Such sensitivity runs in families, as it does in the Waredens. You have a connection with this other world, Matt: your mind forms a mental bridge. Many of our greatest leaders have shared this gift: indeed, I have studied the scriptures, and I believe that Jesus himself shared it.

But, as is so often the case, such gifts bring with them great dangers and responsibilities. I have told you about the special individuals who can form a mental connection with what I have called 'Alternity'.

There are also special places. These places are where the two realms come close together, where Reality and Alternity brush up against one another. These places, or 'Ways' as I call them, are the foci of great power. Often, churches and palaces have been built at or near these places, as new religions unconsciously tap into the power of the ancient.

One such Way exists at Crooked Elms: no doubt that is why the church was built so close to the Waredens' family house. That is how I know you are gifted, Matt: I sent you into the basement to test you, and you suffered – you know you suffered.

This is because of your mental affinity with

Alternity. At a Way, that affinity becomes physical: that mental bridge becomes real. In your head, you carry the key that links Reality and Alternity – a key you must guard. Your talent must be mastered, for the realm of Alternity must never be allowed to spill into the real world: the very fabric of our existence would be destroyed.

Such a tragedy nearly happened a century ago, and again when I was a young man.

It is something that must always be guarded against, and this is where we come to the responsibility to which I referred. The Way is weak, unstable; all kinds of people are drawn to the powers that emanate from these places. Alternity reaches out into their minds and pulls them in. The weak-minded think they can use the powers of Alternity, but in truth it uses *them*, trying to break through into our world. The Way is a weak spot and it must be defended by those who understand. It must be kept shut.

The name Wareden comes from the Old English 'Weardian'. It means guardian, or protector, and that is our role. We are sensitive and we are strong enough to keep the Way closed against those who would open it and let the powers of Alternity loose. Long ago, we were drawn to this Way and now we are bound to it. We are its protectors. This has been our role for generations, and, please God, I hope it always will be.

My dear Matt, I hope you will be able to forgive me: both for my cowardly exit from this place and for those gifts you have inherited from my line. Be strong, Matt. You have to be.

I am tired now. So very tired.

With love,
Gramps

Matt lay back, his head spinning. He could see why Gramps had chosen to write all this down. Spoken aloud, the words would have appeared little more than the ramblings of a demented old man. Spoken aloud, they would have been distorted, misheard, remembered incorrectly.

He stared at the neat writing. This was either totally mad or totally sane. It went against all he had ever understood about the world. He felt as if he was being smothered: everything piling on top of him until it was hard to breathe.

He recalled the strange enclosure in the Crooked Elms churchyard: six families, slaughtered in what the vicar had called 'a night of quite horrific violence'. Matt looked at the letter again: 'such a tragedy nearly happened a century ago . . .'

Nearly? If more than twenty deaths in a single night was 'nearly', what would happen if this Alternity was ever let loose for real, he wondered.

He thought back to the few times he had visited Crooked Elms. As a child he had never been comfortable there: haunted by vivid, frightening dreams, calmed by Gramps' old stories and poems. He remembered going into the basement – only yesterday? it seemed so long ago! – for Gramps' box of books. He remembered the feeling of his feet being stuck in concrete, of being unable to move.

The letter explained it all.

But as he thought about it, and read the letter again and again, he started to question it all. How could such a strange phenomenon be explained by a mere letter? It raised so many questions, so many doubts . . . so many fears.

He struggled to stay awake, suddenly scared of his recurring nightmare. Was he dreaming of Alternity? Was the dream a sign of his 'mental bridge'?

But eventually there was no resisting it, eventually he slept. And dreamt.

9

KIRSTY

He's out running, getting fit for the start of the new football season. Running along Bay Road, heading towards the war memorial and the sea. The sky is a heavy grey, clouds bulging downwards as if about to burst at any second.

There's a metallic grey Volvo up ahead, slowing down, pulling up.

He can see the driver: tall, dark-haired, stooped over the wheel. Leaning over to one side, then straightening, with a mobile phone held to his ear.

Matt raises a hand, tries to call, 'Dad!' but he can't, because suddenly his throat is too tight, too dry. As he approaches the car, the driver replaces the phone and glances into his mirror. His look meets Matt's then moves on. The car pulls out into the road and starts to accelerate.

Matt tries to run harder, but his feet are getting heavier, heavier. The pavement has turned to wet concrete and his feet are sticking, collecting concrete with every step. Getting heavier.

Eventually he reaches the top of the cliff and stares down the grassy slope to the bay in amazement. The sea is red: blood red. And there are things floating on the waves, washed up on to the beach. Arms, feet, heads – all ripped from their bodies by some unimaginably vile force.

He starts to run again, following the road until he comes to Bagshaw Terrace. He turns left, making for town. Faces crowd every window, ghoulish faces with bulging eyes and insane smiles. Every window . . . watching him, smiling. As if they are waiting for something.

This isn't Bathside, he realizes. Although, in a peculiar sense, it *is* Bathside. Where is he, then?

His feet are heavy again, and all he wants to do is stop. But he can't . . . he knows for certain that he can't stop now.

The faces are pressing hard against the windows now, as if sensing his weakness. Hands press at the windows, and he can hear their fingernails – hundreds of fingernails – scratching across the glass, the sound like some mad, warped string section tuning up. Just waiting.

And suddenly he knows where he is. This isn't Bathside, it's an alternative, a Bathside that has never existed but which contains all the darker, twisted Bathsides that *might* have existed if things had been different, if things had been far, far worse.

He's crossing the mental bridge. He's out jogging in Alternity, and his feet are getting heavier and heavier again.

He stares at all the ghoulish, eager faces.

He'll have to stop running soon. He won't be able to go on for much longer. He'll have to . . .

He woke, his body soaked in sweat, his head aching as if someone had been trying to break out of his skull with a pneumatic drill. He sat up straight, hugging himself, willing the mad images to go away, willing the pain to stop.

He was going insane, he knew. Almost every night now, he was having these dark, terrifying dreams. Even now that he had some kind of explanation – even if it was one that transformed everything he had ever understood about the world – he feared that it would end in madness.

How had Gramps lasted so long if he had suffered like this, he wondered. And how did a child of Kirsty's age cope with it? Little wonder she had so many 'turns', as Aunt Carol called them.

These thoughts offered a morsel of comfort to him: Kirsty survived, Gramps had lived with it for more than eighty years. There must be a way of coping. He remembered the letter, Gramps' phrase: *your talent must be mastered.*

He had to find some way of controlling it, whatever *it* was. He had to master this gift, this affliction. The alternative, he knew, was insanity. Or maybe something worse.

The following afternoon presented Matt with his first opportunity to learn. It was the first time he had been alone with Kirsty for more than a few seconds, the first time he had had the chance to talk to her.

Vince and Mike were at work, his mother and aunt were at the hospital with Gramps, and Tina had gone to a friend's birthday party. That had come as a surprise to Matt: he couldn't imagine Tina having any kind of a life outside the small circle of her family. Perhaps they weren't very close friends, he decided. She hadn't been at all keen to go to this party, after all, but Carol had insisted. 'You accepted the invitation,' she told her. 'You have to learn to meet your obligations. You're going to go to this party, my girl, and what's more, you're going to enjoy it.'

Kirsty seemed to be trying to avoid him. There were just the two of them in the house, yet he didn't see her for nearly an hour. She was up in her room, he guessed.

He settled down at the end of the sofa with one of his grandparents' old photograph albums. This one dated back to the early 1950s. Gran and Gramps would have been about the same age as his parents were now, he realized. Next to each of the pictures was a label, written in his grandmother's flowing script, identifying the place and time. *Alhambra Palace, Granada, July 12th 1953. Toledo, August 4th 1953. The Prado, Madrid, August 6th 1953.*

The small girl in the pictures must be Carol, he thought. The baby would have been his mother. His grandparents looked so contented, so at one with their world. The young doctor and his wife.

It seemed like a golden age to Matt. He wondered what it was really like. What had been going through the mind of that man? What fears, what worries? What night terrors did he endure?

Perhaps that was why he had travelled so much: distance offering the only respite from the madness, and the danger. Had he been running away?

Matt looked up as the TV leapt into life. Kirsty had come into the room without a sound, and now she was setting up one of her video games. She met his look briefly, then turned away.

'Hi, Kirsty,' he said.

'Hello.' Her voice was small, uncertain. Suddenly, he knew that Tina must have spoken to her before going out, warning her to steer clear of cousin Matthew. Was she deliberately going against her sister's wishes by coming down here now, he wondered. Was this her little act of rebellion?

Soon she became quite absorbed in the game, her eyes wide and fixed on the screen. It was a racing game, he saw, not the usual battle game that she played with Tina. He grinned as his cousin's small body flexed and leaned into every corner.

He let her finish the circuit before saying anything. 'Not bad,' he said then. 'Where did you finish?'

She looked at him shyly again. 'It was just a practice lap,' she said.

He nodded.

'Tina doesn't like racing,' she went on, as if she was gaining in confidence. 'She likes Kombat. She always does better than me at Kombat. Do you play?'

He shook his head. 'Not much,' he told her. 'I've got a Game Boy, but not here. It's at . . . at home.'

She offered him the handset. 'Here. Have a go. It's easy, really.'

He put the album aside and moved across to sit on the floor. Taking the controls, he studied them carefully.

'This one's the speed. This is your brakes . . .'

He sat quietly as she explained. She reset the game and, finally, let him have a go. He made sure he crashed early on and sat back, shaking his head. 'You made it look easy,' he said. 'But that corner just came out of nowhere.'

She laughed. 'I did that first time, too,' she said. 'You get used to it, I suppose. Another go?'

He shook his head and handed the controls back to his cousin. 'Nah,' he said, 'I'll leave it to the professionals.'

She was pretty much like any other seven-year-old, he thought. A bit shy, a bit submissive to the demands of her mother and older sister, maybe a bit mischievous. He was wondering how to shift the talk to more serious matters when Kirsty did it for him.

'Are you really going to be living here now?' she asked. 'Until you're a grown-up, I mean.'

He shook his head. 'Not that long,' he said. 'Just a few days. Mum needs to sort herself out, then when she knows what she's doing I can make my own decisions.' It sounded very uncomplicated, put like that.

'Tina says you're a . . . a destabilizing influence. She says you're making the bad dreams.'

Matt had to stop himself from staring at Kirsty in surprise – he couldn't afford to put her off now. 'Do you believe her?' he asked. '*Am* I making bad dreams?'

She tipped her head to one side, finding the confidence to study his face as she replied. 'You're certainly doing something,' she said. 'I've had more funny turns since you came than I did all of last year. And I am having more bad dreams, too.'

He remembered what Gramps had said in his letter about dark powers emanating from the Way, about mental bridges and the need to master the gift. Was his mere presence stirring up dark forces? Was he really making Kirsty ill? No wonder Tina hated him.

'I'm not doing anything deliberately,' he said. 'And you seem OK now, don't you?'

She seemed to accept this argument. He plunged on, determined to learn as much as he could from this rare conversation. 'I've been having bad dreams, too.' He watched her closely as he spoke. 'Frightening dreams, about a world that's not quite like this – a place that's scary, where you see some horrific things. There's always a terrible sense of doom, a feeling that some horrifying, monstrous *thing* is just out of the picture, waiting for me . . . always waiting for me.'

Kirsty was nodding in recognition. 'Alternity,' she said softly.

She knew its name, then. He wasn't sure what this proved, except that Gramps must have spoken to her at some time, perhaps in an effort to help her master her gift, to control her 'turns'. Gramps was a doctor, after all; Carol was bound to have turned to him when Kirsty had started showing signs of the family affliction.

'Did your mother give you a letter from Gramps?' he asked.

She shook her head. She clearly didn't understand what he was referring to. He had been fairly certain that Carol wouldn't have passed on the letters Gramps had written the day before. So Kirsty must have learnt about Alternity some time earlier, then.

'Have you dreamed of . . . Alternity very much?' he asked her.

'It started when I was four,' she said. 'I wouldn't go to bed at night unless Tina was with me and the light was on and Mum was sitting on the landing playing her guitar.'

She seemed quite proud of this, Matt thought.

She paused, then went on. 'One time we visited Gran and Gramps and I had a turn. Gramps looked after me. He told me stories and taught me old poems that would help me close the doors in my brain.'

Matt suddenly recalled those rare childhood visits to Crooked Elms when he was little. Gramps had always liked telling him old stories – King Arthur,

Joan of Arc, Beowulf – and old poems. Matt hadn't understood them, but they had soothed him. Now he remembered quite distinctly how Gramps had used the poems to settle him and help him sleep at night. 'Words have a magic,' the old man had said. 'They work the locks to the doors of the mind.'

Kirsty continued, 'He told me that it was very special to be able to see into Alternity, but that it was scary as well, and that I should always keep my dreams locked up in a special place.'

Her look became distant, just then. For a moment, Matt had the horrible feeling that he had somehow triggered another of her turns. What was he supposed to do if that happened? He had done a first-aid course through the football club, but that hardly prepared you for dealing with this kind of thing.

But she was thinking of Gramps. 'Is he really going to be all right?' she asked. 'Is he going to get better again?'

'Sure,' Matt said. 'He's being looked after. He's getting better.'

'Mum said you saved his life.'

He shook his head. 'I didn't do anything much,' he said.

'You can't really be as bad as Tina says if you saved Gramps' life, can you?'

A short time later, Matt heard the front door open and, immediately after that, the sound of his aunt's voice.

She came into the front room, followed by Matt's mother and then by Tina – they must have picked her up from the party after leaving the hospital.

Instantly, Matt was aware that he was still sitting on the floor next to Kirsty. Tina stared at the two of them, at first in surprise and then with narrowing, angry eyes.

Matt ignored her. He had done nothing wrong. 'How's Gramps?' he asked his mother.

She looked away and he knew something was amiss. Then she looked at him and tried to smile. 'Oh,' she said, 'about as well as one could hope, really. He's an old man. He's very lucky, really.'

Meaning, of course, that he wasn't nearly as well as she had expected him to be.

'How long will he be in hospital?' He was aware that they wouldn't want to say too much in front of Kirsty, but he wanted to know as much as possible.

'They're keeping him in for now,' said Carol. 'He's been through a lot for a man of his age. We have to take things day by day.'

'But he will come home, won't he?' asked Kirsty.

Carol nodded and smiled her brittle smile. 'Of course he will, darling. The doctors just need to make sure everything's working properly, that's all.'

'He's going to die, isn't he?' Kirsty's voice was rising, becoming shrill. 'Just like Gran!'

Tina rushed to her sister's side, forcing herself into the narrow space between Kirsty and Matt.

Matt got to his feet and went to pick up the

photograph album, determined not to let Tina's behaviour disturb him.

But then, when he glanced back at the two girls, he saw that Kirsty had frozen, her eyes focused on some hazy middle distance. Tina held her sister's head against her shoulder and rocked her back and forth.

'Mum,' she said quietly. Then, as Carol hurried across to the two of them, Tina turned her hard stare on Matt.

Kirsty was having one of her turns, and it was all Matt's fault.

Tina's eyes burned into him. Even when he looked away, he was aware of her eyes, the intensity of her anger.

He sat down and started to leaf through the album once again.

10

OUTSIDERS

The following afternoon, Matt went with Aunt Carol to see Gramps in hospital.

He had spent the morning in town with his mother. She was buying a suit to wear for job interviews, and for some reason she wanted Matt to be with her. She seemed to be trying to impress on him how seriously she was taking what she called 'the next big step'. This afternoon she had appointments with the town's three employment agencies.

The core of the hospital was a cluster of tall, Victorian, red-brick buildings, the grounds of which had been steadily filled in with modern concrete annexes. Stoham Ward was on the first floor of one of the older buildings, with windows that looked out across the flat roofs of a neighbouring block.

They paused in the doorway and Matt surveyed the ranks of beds along either wall. Ancient, grey-faced men lay staring at the ceiling, waiting to die. Others, just as old, sat in chairs by their beds, studying the pages of newspapers or large-print books, or talking to visitors. In a side room, a small semicircle of aged men sat watching daytime TV.

Gramps was one of the patients lying in bed. Matt swallowed, unprepared for the sudden rush of emotion he felt.

'Like I said in the car,' Carol told him, 'Gramps is very ill. You mustn't expect too much from him.'

But then Matt noticed that Gramps was not alone. The vicar of Crooked Elms was sitting by his bed, leaning forward, talking earnestly.

The vicar stood as Matt and Carol approached. 'Ah,' he said, 'visitors.'

Gramps lay motionless, but Matt saw his eyes move slowly from the vicar to his new visitors and back again.

'Carol,' said the young vicar. 'And this is . . .?'

'Matt,' said Carol. 'My nephew.'

The vicar nodded. 'We have met before,' he said. 'I didn't realize you were a Wareden, Matt.'

There was something about the way he said the name that Matt didn't like – the reference to his family name, the too-familiar use of his *first* name.

Matt shrugged, said nothing.

'I hope you don't mind,' the vicar continued, addressing Carol. 'I was visiting another gentleman of my parish and I couldn't help but notice your father.'

'Of course not, David,' Carol said quickly. 'It's very kind of you.' To Matt she added, 'David has always taken an interest in our family – he visited Gramps a lot, before . . .'

The vicar smiled awkwardly. 'We miss him in the village,' he said. 'I hadn't realized he was here. He asked me to keep an eye on his house. I've been doing that anyway – Neighbourhood Watch and all that – but I assured him I would continue. Mrs Wareden was always a regular member of our congregation . . .' He hesitated, as if aware that he was treading in a delicate area, then plunged on. 'I hope your family is keeping well, Mrs Smith. How are your lovely daughters?'

It seemed that he couldn't stop talking, now that he had started, but Carol managed to get rid of him after a few minutes.

Gramps watched them all the time through heavy-lidded eyes. He had probably been sedated, Matt guessed.

'How are you, Gramps?' he asked tentatively.

His grandfather just stared at him, and Matt wondered if the old man blamed him for stopping him from killing himself.

'Dad?' said Carol. 'Can you hear us, Dad?'

Gramps licked his lips, then murmured in a soft whisper, 'I can hear you, Carol.' But he was still staring at Matt.

Matt wanted to tell him that he had read the letter, and that he understood. He wanted to tell him that he almost wished he had just walked past that open door, so that Gramps wasn't found until much later. But then, he wondered, why had Gramps left the door open, if he hadn't wanted to be found?

'Everybody sends their love,' said Carol, unaware of the currents passing between Gramps and Matt.

'We're all praying for you, Dad. We all want you to get better quickly.'

Gramps managed to nod. Then he closed his eyes. A few seconds later, he opened them again. 'I'm tired,' he said. 'So tired.'

Matt couldn't stay. He couldn't take the accusing look in his grandfather's eyes. He made his excuses, telling Carol he'd meet her at the car.

A few moments later he stepped out into the sunlight. There was a scented garden here, with a fountain and some plastic seats. Over to one side a young man was pushing an elderly woman in a wheelchair, both looking politely bored by the other's company.

The vicar was there too, sitting on a white bench. He rose to his feet when Matt emerged. He must have been waiting.

He nodded and said, 'Your grandfather – he's not a happy man. If there's anything I can do . . .'

'Thanks,' said Matt. 'But we're OK.'

'There have always been Waredens in Crooked Elms.' The man seemed hesitant, yet clearly he had something to say to Matt. 'The village seems odd without them. Unprotected, I suppose.'

Matt squinted at the man. His choice of words . . . How much did he know? 'You seem to know a lot about my family,' he said.

The vicar smiled. 'It is an interesting parish and there's something of the amateur historian in me. When I came to Crooked Elms, six years ago, your grandfather was very hostile and I became determined to find out why. It emerged that he had had a dispute with one of my predecessors a long, long time ago.'

'What kind of dispute?'

'The Reverend Harold Allbright was a charismatic figure – very persuasive, very forceful. And, it emerged, he was a very corrupt individual: driven by the Devil, although your grandfather would never use such language. For a time he and your grandfather were friends, but their relationship soured.'

The words from Gramps' letter came back to Matt just then: 'such tragedy nearly happened a century ago, and again when I was a young man'. This Devil-driven vicar . . . had he been drawn in and corrupted by the power of Alternity? Was this the incident that had taken place when Gramps was a young man?

'What happened?'

'Your grandfather accused Allbright of certain dark practices and turned the villagers against him,' said the vicar. 'Those possessed by darkness are readily discarded when they are no longer useful. My predecessor died while still a young man and his body lies in a simple grave in the churchyard at Crooked Elms.'

The vicar was standing close to Matt now. Too close. He put a hand on Matt's shoulder. 'I don't pretend to understand what happened in my parish,' he said. 'But I know that it is a special place and that your grandfather is a special man. I'm praying for his recovery, Matt. Praying with all my strength.'

Back at the house, Vince was working on his car. He was lying on one side on the pavement, folding sheets of newspaper around the front nearside wheel, preparing to spray a filled dent on the wing.

'Not working?' asked Carol, as they passed him.

He glared at her. 'Told you,' he said. 'It was only short term. We cleared the site this morning.'

'Have you been to the Job Centre? If I'd known, I'd have asked Jill to have a look – she was going there this afternoon.'

'Jobs don't grow on trees,' Vince said, sitting up. 'The sort of thing I do – you get it through word of mouth, not from cards put up in the Job Centre.'

'You mean casual, cash-in-hand jobs that last a few days?' Carol said sarcastically. 'I'm sorry, I got it wrong. I was talking about real jobs. Ones with a bit of security, ones with prospects.'

Vince yawned loudly into the back of his hand. Then he nodded across at a cardboard box balanced on the wall. 'Here, Matt,' he said. 'Chuck us the paint, will you?'

Carol marched into the house, and Matt took an aerosol can out of the box and passed it to his cousin.

Vince shook the can and it rattled loudly, startling Matt. 'Old cow,' Vince muttered.

Matt leant back against the wall. The vicar's

words had disturbed him more deeply than he liked to admit. He tried to put them out of his mind. Instead, he studied his cousin. Fussing over his car like this, Vince didn't look like the sort of person Gramps would warn against, but then Matt had seen the other side of him, too. 'Sounded like you've had that discussion before,' he said.

Vince turned to his car and, holding the nozzle a short distance from the surface, started to spray. 'Been to see the old goat, have you?'

Matt nodded. 'He was awake for a few minutes,' he said. Gramps had been unconscious for most of the previous day, his mother had told him. 'He didn't seem too pleased to see us.'

Vince's hand moved methodically from side to side, and soon the patch was completely covered. 'He'll be loving it,' he said. 'All those nurses, doing everything he wants. That's probably why he did it. He'd have done it properly if he'd really wanted to top himself, wouldn't he?'

'You think so?'

'Course I do,' said Vince. 'He's a doctor, isn't he? He's just like a spoilt kid, chucking the toys out of his cot to get attention. He's had it all his own way for far too long.'

Vince tossed the aerosol across the pavement into the box, then started to remove a strip of masking tape that was holding a piece of paper over the nearest headlight.

'You heard from your dad, yet, have you?' he asked.

Matt shook his head. 'No,' he said. 'He's hardly going to call *here*, is he?'

'Why don't you call him, then?'

He had, but he didn't want to talk about it. Certainly not to Vince. He'd tried this morning, but had only reached the answering machine, yet again.

'I don't see why I should be the one to do everything,' Matt said. 'Neither of them let me know what was going on until they had to.'

Vince nodded. 'I know how you feel,' he said. 'You want to hear a story, do you? When Carol got pregnant with Tina, everything changed round here. I didn't understand it: they were suddenly happy, they stopped arguing, they started talking behind shut doors so I couldn't hear.

'But they never told *me*. Sounds stupid, but I really thought she was just getting fat – I was only six. They didn't know how to tell me, because suddenly they wished they'd never taken me, they wished they'd just waited a bit longer. Eventually I worked it out for myself, and I hated them for it. All they had to do was *tell* me.'

Vince's intensity reminded Matt of the morning at Crooked Elms when he had slashed his own arm, just to prove how serious he was.

'Parents are like that,' said Vince. 'They don't trust you. You've got to learn not to trust them in return – when you've done that, it's all OK.' Then he smiled. 'You and me, we're just the same,' he concluded. 'Outsiders. Outsiders in our own family.'

*

Later, Matt headed upstairs. He wanted to be alone. He needed to think things through – as if that would make any difference. He already knew what his options were: stay here with his warped family and make a new start with his mother, or return to Norwich, where none of this madness had ever intruded. His friends were in Norwich, and his father; but did he really want that, he wondered. It would be running away, he knew. Perhaps running away from something he would have to deal with later: if there really was any truth in his grandfather's claims, then he knew that now was the time to deal with it, to learn control.

He went into his room and shut the door. Leaning with his back against it, he closed his eyes and tried to relax. He wouldn't gain anything by letting it all get to him like this; he had to stay cool.

There was a strange smell in the room. Briny, decaying, like mouldering seaweed, only somehow more foul than that. For a moment he couldn't place it, then he remembered where he had encountered it before: in his mother's room at Bagshaw Terrace.

The dead seagull!

He looked round the room, but there was no sign of it. The last one had been in a plastic bag – but this room was *full* of carrier bags and boxes! He made himself calm down.

He closed his eyes again and tried to picture the room as it had been this morning. There would be a new bag somewhere, or signs of disturbance.

He opened his eyes, looked around. Nothing seemed to have been moved, nothing added. He went across and opened the window. The two of them were playing, down in the garden: two sisters, chasing each other around, such an innocent scene.

He turned back to the room and thought. He had to be methodical.

He stripped his bedding back, then peered underneath the camp bed. Nothing.

He sat on the bed and tried again to look for anything that had been moved. Again he had no luck. He tried to work out if there was a part of the room where the smell was strongest, but there was not. He started poking about in the bags and boxes, cautiously at first, then gaining steadily in confidence.

A quarter of an hour later, he gave up the search.

His first inclination was to go downstairs and confront the little demon, demand to know what she had done to his room. But he knew that would achieve little, other than giving her the satisfaction of knowing she had upset him.

He went across to the window and looked down into the garden. Tina and Kirsty had stopped playing now. They were sitting, side by side, on the stone bench at the far end of the garden. Kirsty was hunched forward, her head bent low over a glossy magazine. Tina was sitting back with her feet on the bench, her knees tucked up under her chin. She was fiddling with something – a ball of wool, a small doll, a dead mouse, for all Matt knew – and every so often she would pause and look up at his open window.

He turned away and found his current book on the floor by the camp bed. He picked it up, then straightened. Either the open window had cleared the smell or he was getting used to it. Or perhaps he had been imagining things.

He went downstairs.

'Guess what?'

Matt looked up. His mother stood in the doorway. She was wearing her grey interview suit. She looked happy, her cheeks were flushed, her eyes bright and dancing. He couldn't remember the last time she had looked like this.

'You and Dad are getting back together again?'

Instantly, her expression changed: the familiar hard lines appeared across her forehead, her mouth twitched as she stopped herself from replying. She reached up and patted the hair she had tied back neatly this morning.

Matt returned his gaze to the pages of his book.

'I've got a job,' she said in a tightly controlled voice. 'I thought you might be interested.'

He looked up again, nodded. 'Well done,' he said. Then he relented and added, 'I mean it: well done. You didn't hang about.'

She smiled and came into the room. 'Accounts Assistant at Sperry and Neeskens, shipping agents. Temporary cover for staff sickness. Starting tomorrow. I know, I should be looking for something

114

better, but at least it's something. A temporary job's often a good way in, for when something more permanent comes along.'

'That's what they told you, is it?'

She laughed. 'That's exactly what they told me,' she said. 'And I really believed them at the time, too. Who knows? Something may come of it. At least I'll be in a better position for when something better does come up – I've been out of the job market for so long, I need to prove I can still hack it. And it means some money in the bank, it means we can look for somewhere to live.'

Her expression was becoming more serious, more determined.

'I'm going to make this work, Matt. At last it seems as if things are starting to fall into place. This is our chance to make a new start. You wait and see, Matt. Just you wait and see.'

It was finally, really beginning to sink in. Despite all the talk, despite all he had thought, none of it had been real. But now . . . she really *was* going to stay in Bathside. She really was making a fresh start.

He lowered his head and stared blankly at the pages of his book.

Eventually he heard a sound from the doorway, and when he looked up he saw that she had gone. To pass on her good news to the others, no doubt.

He couldn't help smiling at that: Tina, for one, was going to be delighted.

11

TINA

He'd thought Tina was strange. He'd thought she was over-protective. He'd even thought she was mad.

But he had never thought she would try to kill him.

Late the next morning, he was heading downstairs. She was on the first-floor landing, watching him approach.

She was smiling. And he knew why. He had been forced to sleep with his window wide open in an attempt to conquer the foetid smell of decay, grateful for the warmth that lingered late into the summer night, woken early by the cool breeze that had come in from the sea just before dawn.

'Did you sleep well?' she asked in an innocent tone.

He nodded. 'Fine,' he said. 'Never better. In fact, I'm getting to like that room.' He smiled broadly at her, and added, 'You know, I'm really beginning to think of it as *my* room. Home sweet home. Could stay here forever – there's plenty of space, after all: it's a big house. What do you think?'

Her smile was fixed rigidly on her face now, making Matt think of the smile her mother determinedly wore whenever things became difficult for her.

'Really?' she said hesitantly. 'I thought . . .'

'I was joking,' said Matt. 'J-O-K-E. Look it up in the dictionary, if you know how. You can relax. We'll be going, sooner or later.' But then he couldn't resist pushing her, and he added, 'About six weeks, I reckon. Time for us to save up for a deposit on a place to rent.'

The look on her face was a reward in itself: the sheer rage, as if she was about to burst like an over-filled balloon.

He smiled, and went on, 'Still, it'll be nice, won't it? It'll give us time to get to know each other. You, me, Kirsty. Plenty of time to become friends. Kirsty showed me how to play her racing game – the one you don't like. Maybe I'll race her some time.' He continued, enjoying himself: 'And even then, when we find a place, we'll always be near by. We'll be able to pop in whenever we feel like it. Won't that be nice? We might even be neighbours . . .'

He turned away from her, thrilling at the mad, frustrated look on her face. He would go downstairs, maybe go out for a run or something.

He took the first step down, then heard a soft sound. It was a footstep on the landing, close behind him.

Then he felt a sudden push in his back, enough to knock him forward, off balance.

He put a foot out, trying to place it on one of the

steps to steady himself, but he was tipping forward too fast.

He raised his hands and grabbed at the banister, but he couldn't grip it, he was twisting, falling out of control.

He tucked his arms into his body, hands in front of his face, as he crashed into the stairs. A sudden bolt of pain stabbed through his body, then a numb blackness started to spread through his head, as the world went round and round, out of control.

He lay on his back, finally come to rest. It felt like hours must have passed. Days, weeks.

His head was pounding and the left side of his face felt numb, smothered with a strangely unfocused pain. His ribs ached and his left ankle felt peculiar. He shifted the leg, relieved that he could move it, that it was not broken as he had at first feared.

He opened his eyes and gradually the world came into focus.

Tina was halfway down the stairs, her face pale, tears streaming down her cheeks. Suddenly, Matt wondered if this was the last thing his grandmother had seen.

He blinked rapidly, trying to clear his blurred vision.

Tina looked shocked, as if horrified at what had just happened . . . what she had just done. 'Are you . . . are you . . .' Even now, she couldn't bring herself to say more than that.

He pulled himself up to a sitting position, ignoring the protests from his body, sensing the anger building.

As she came down the stairs, he scrambled to his feet, driven by an inhuman fury. He took a big step towards her, grabbed a fistful of her hair and jerked her head back sharply.

The two of them fell over on to the stairs, Matt on top of his cousin, pinning her down, twisting her hair in his fist.

He had never been so angry in all his life.

He was going to get some sense out of her. Going to get the truth. And he was going to hurt her.

'Hey!'

Hands grabbed him, pinning his arms tightly against his sides, forcing him to loosen his grip on Tina.

'Hey.' The voice was softer now, calming.

He looked back, over his shoulder, into Vince's puzzled face. He slumped. The rage was gone, and for a moment he regretted its passing.

He looked down. Tina was sobbing, struggling to squirm free.

He shook himself out of Vince's grip, then stood up and backed away. He felt ashamed – guilty, even – and he was angry at feeling like that.

'She tried to kill me,' he muttered.

Vince looked from Matt to Tina, and he started to smile. Then he started to laugh.

He clapped Matt on the arm. 'Excellent!' he said, when he managed to control himself. 'You guys really crack me up. Come on, Matt. Let's get out of here, before war breaks out.'

And he led Matt towards the front door, still laughing and shaking his head. 'You guys,' he said again. Then: 'What a family . . .'

12

CONFRONTATION

'Now are you going to tell me what that was all about?'

They were down on the Promenade, Vince throwing stones into the surf, Matt watching a ferry slide across the horizon. All around them the holidaymakers carried on, going about their business as normal. It was another world.

Only a matter of minutes had passed, yet it all seemed so long ago. Already the pain in his ribs and face had eased, and his ankle only hurt when he put his full weight on it. He made himself remember how he had felt: the anger . . . the anger had been an alien feeling, as if he had been temporarily possessed by some ancient spirit.

She had tried to kill him.

'She's mad,' he said. It was difficult to put into words what had just happened. Difficult to express his rage. 'She pushed me down the stairs. Came up behind me, caught me unawares. I could have broken my neck.'

Vince nodded. 'I never really thought she'd have

it in her,' he said, in an admiring tone. 'I never thought she'd have the bottle.'

Matt stared at Vince's pale features. 'You don't seem all that surprised,' he said.

Vince shrugged. 'Like you say: the kid's mad, isn't she? One hundred per cent certifiable. What do you expect? You shouldn't have given her the chance. And another thing: you're going to have to be a bit more subtle, OK? If you beat her brains out, like you just tried to do, then everyone knows it's you. Nobody ever gets anything by dumb revenge.'

He laughed, then hurled another rock out into the waves. 'What a family,' he said again. He pulled a packet of cigarettes out of his leather jacket and lit one, then turned to Matt again. 'Why'd she push you, then?'

'She hates me,' said Matt. 'She always has. Ever since we came here she's been trying to get us to leave. She's just over-protective, I suppose. She blames me for Kirsty's funny turns.' He stopped abruptly, but it was too late to retract what he had just said. He remembered Gramps' warning about Vince: *You should be careful of that one. He doesn't know how dangerous he is . . .*

'Yeah?' said Vince, watching him carefully. 'Why does she think that, then?'

Was Vince trying to trap him into saying things he shouldn't? But then he had just stopped Matt from attacking Tina . . . Sometimes, despite everything, Vince seemed the sanest person in this mad household.

'It's like you said, that day we went out to Gramps' house,' said Matt, not sure how much he should say, how much Vince already knew. 'This family's blighted: there's a madness, a weakness. Tina thinks that just by being here I'm somehow making Kirsty worse – that's what Kirsty told me, anyway. Gramps has taught Kirsty how to control the madness, but she says that because I don't have this control, I'm disturbing things.'

Vince was nodding slowly. 'You think that's true?'

'Do you?'

'Like I told you,' he said, 'you and Kirsty are the same. That day you blacked out in the basement, you looked just like Kirsty does when she has a turn: frozen rigid, your eyes staring. It happens because you're sensitive to the place, so why shouldn't it happen because you're sensitive to each other too?' He paused, then said, 'So Tina doesn't like it, eh?'

Matt shook his head. 'She says I'm a destabilizing influence. Until I came along she was in charge, but she knows she can't control me.'

'It's more than that, though,' said Vince. 'She's missed out. This sensitivity runs in families, doesn't it? But not everyone inherits it. Kirsty's got it, you've got it. So where does that leave Tina? She's just an ordinary girl, and she hates it.'

Vince was envious. He was talking about this sensitivity as if it were a gift, Matt realized – just as Gramps had called it a gift. Maybe he could answer some of Matt's questions, if only he could work out how to phrase them.

Vince broke the silence. 'You thought I was the mad one when I talked about all this stuff before. Remember? So what's changed your mind? Is it because you spoke to Kirsty? Or has something else happened?'

Vince was looking out across the bay and Matt couldn't read his expression. Should he trust him, he wondered. He had said so much already, he had little to lose by revealing a bit more. *Your talent must be mastered*, Gramps had said. But before he did that, he had to understand it first. He reached into his pocket for the letter. Slowly he withdrew it, unfolded it, handed it to Vince.

Vince studied the letter, nodding occasionally, smiling. When he had finished, he peered at Matt through his dark fringe. 'That's what she called it, too. Alternity.' He stared out to sea through narrowed eyes and drew deeply on his cigarette.

'Who?' Matt asked, but Vince didn't respond.

Finally he said, 'So now you believe. The big question is, how are you going to learn how to handle it?'

Matt reached out and took the letter from Vince's grasp. 'How do you know about all this?' he said. 'Gramps wouldn't have told you.'

Vince shook his head. 'Like I said before: I've studied these things. I've been stuck with this family for most of my life – I've had to make sense of all the weird things that have gone on. Gran was the only one who ever trusted me. None of the others will have anything to do with me, but she was OK. She thought I had a right to know why things were like this. She explained a lot, but not everything. I had to work some of it out for myself. Fill in the gaps. If you know where to look and who to speak to, you can find out all kinds of things.

'The old goat uses different language to describe it, but the kind of thing he's talking about has been known to mankind for thousands of years. There have always been special places, and special people who know how to use them.'

'Gramps didn't say anything about *using* the Way,' said Matt, thinking of all those graves, the lives lost when things had gone wrong in 1898. 'He talked about defending it, or protecting it . . .'

Vince laughed. 'Even though he has some of the sensitivity,' he said, 'he's just like Tina: scared of change, convinced that any development will be bad.'

'That makes sense to me.'

'Think about it! Why have you got this gift, if not to use it? Generations of gifted people have used their skills – healers, great leaders of men. Think of all the power just waiting to be tapped, and controlled – you must be aware of it, you must have felt it. Even I've felt it, and I'm not as sensitive as you. Read between the lines of the old goat's letter, Matt: he's telling you that you're in charge. You're a Wareden: a guardian – the Way through to Alternity is in your care, along with all the powers that, as the letter says, "emanate from this place". It's up to you, Matt, to use it however you choose: in the letter he calls it tapping into the "power of the ancient". Think of all the things you could do with that power!'

Vince was staring at him, grinning excitedly. 'It's up to you, Matt,' he said, 'whether you use the powers you've been given, or whether you just turn away from them like your grandfather did.

'But one thing's certain: you've got to learn to control them. Otherwise you'll just crack up, or Alternity will take you by surprise one day and destroy you.'

Matt knew Vince was telling him the truth: he had come to exactly the same conclusion himself. He had to master his sensitivity, before *it* mastered *him*. 'But how?' he said. 'How do I learn to control it?'

'Confrontation,' said Vince, still grinning. 'The only way to master Alternity is to confront it . . .'

Matt sat in the car, still not quite believing he was here, not quite believing he had let Vince talk him into coming to Crooked Elms. He wasn't ready for this. He was too young to handle it.

But what about Kirsty, a voice inside his head reminded him. She had been only four when her sensitivity had awakened and Gramps had taught her how to cope.

Vince was watching him with dark, intense eyes. 'Are you going to learn to control it?' he asked softly. 'Or are you going to let it control you?'

Matt ignored him, remembering the last time he had been here.

Vince took the bunch of keys from his jacket pocket and jangled them in front of Matt's face. 'Come on, Matt,' he said. 'You're different to the others. I noticed that when you were here in March. You're tougher than the rest of them. You're not the sort to bottle out, are you, Matt? Are you?'

Matt reached for the door and pushed it open. He wasn't going to let Vince bully him into anything: this was his own decision, something only he could do. Something he had to confront. He thought of the dreams, of how they had become steadily more intense and disturbing – Alternity reaching out for him, trying to take a hold of his mind, he felt sure of that now.

He had to face up to it. The alternative was to lose his mind.

Outside, he leant against the car and stared at the house's front door. 'So what do I do?' he asked, as Vince came round to join him.

'Reach out,' said Vince. 'Can you feel it yet? The old goat called it an affinity with Alternity, a mental bridge. A Way is the place where that mental bridge becomes real. He said that in your head you have a key that links the real with the alternative. You just have to learn how to use it. Can you feel it yet?'

Matt could feel it, all right. Something just beyond his normal perception, beyond seeing or hearing. Beyond reality.

Vince opened the door and stepped inside. He paused in the hallway and looked back at Matt, his pale features ghostlike in the shadowy interior.

Matt swallowed, but the dry lump in his throat wouldn't go away. He made his feet move and followed Vince inside.

He stared at the door leading down to the basement. 'That's where it is, isn't it?' he said. It made sense. Gramps said that people tended to build churches and shrines at these special places – the Way had been here before these buildings, so they must be rooted in the ground, in the bedrock below the soil.

The basement.

Matt stepped towards the door but was stopped by Vince's hand on his arm.

'Remember last time?' Vince said. 'You just blacked out. Where's the sense in that?'

'But I can control it, now that I know what's likely to happen. Gramps could. Kirsty can – at least some of the time.' He tried to think. 'The key's in my head. That's what the letter said. I have to work it out.'

'Is there anything the old boy told you that gives any kind of a hint about how you get this control? What does Kirsty do? It must be something significant, but also something simple enough for a small girl to use. What does she do, Matt? Think!'

He remembered Kirsty's words: *Gramps looked after me. He told me stories and taught me old poems that would help me close the doors in my brain*. Something special, yet simple enough for a small girl to use: those old poems that Gramps loved! *Words have a magic*, Gramps had told him, years ago. *They work the locks to the doors of the mind*. All those years ago, Gramps had been preparing him for this!

Something about the doors of the righteous – Gramps had taught him that one when he was small: he had used it to help settle him at night. Matt hadn't understood it, but he had found that the strange words seemed to shut out the dreams, the night terrors that had plagued his first stay in this house.

The doors of the righteous . . . what else was it?

He was on the right track, he realized. Even thinking about those words was sending a wave of reassurance through his mind: calming him, helping him think. How had it gone?

'You know, don't you, Matt?'

He nodded. 'I think so,' he said. 'Special words. If only I can remember them.'

'Say them out loud, Matt. Assert yourself.'

He started hesitantly.

'Never the doors of the righteous be breached.' It was coming back to him!

'The minds of the pure are our shield,
   Protect us from evil, protect us from fear . . .'

What was the rest of it? 'Shine light where the shadow concealed.'

Silence. A stillness so absolute it was as if time itself had paused.

He stepped towards the basement door. 'I'm going down there,' he said. 'Down to where it's strongest.'

He went down the stone stairs.

The basement was the same as before: piles of boxes and accumulated junk retreating into the shadows. He walked on a concrete floor, next to smoothed brick walls that glistened with moisture. The basement was lit by a pool of light from a single bare bulb suspended from the middle of the low ceiling.

He turned around, passing through 360 degrees. This place felt ancient, he realized – a chamber in the ground that was far older than the house itself. He remembered last time: how his feet had grown so heavy, just as in the dreams. How he had been almost unable to move, struggling to drag himself across the floor. How he had finally collapsed on the stairs, where Vince had found him.

The heat struck him first, an intense wave passing over him, as if he was about to faint.

Then it was suddenly a huge effort simply to breathe.

'The words, Matt.' Vince had followed him, he realized.

He struggled to turn his head, to look at his cousin.

'Never the doors of the righteous be breached.'

He filled his lungs as the weight momentarily lifted.

'The minds of the pure are our shield,
Protect us from evil, protect us from fear,
Shine light where the shadow concealed.'

'Confront it, Matt! Assert yourself!'

He peered at Vince's white face, his staring eyes. How?

The words, he thought. The power is in the words. He should *change* the words, then. Take control of them. Twist them, shift them, reverse them. As soon as he thought that, it seemed the right thing to do . . .

'Never the shield of our minds be breached.' He didn't know what he was saying, or why he was saying it . . . The words just seemed to rearrange themselves on his tongue.

So easy.

So tempting.

'Shine shadow, where light had concealed.'

The basement was shifting, rearranging itself, just as the words were doing.

'Protect us from evil, protect us from fear –'

The air was wavering, so that it was like looking through a lens, like looking into a distorting mirror.

'Shine shadow, where light had concealed!'

A shimmering disc appeared, about two metres in front of him, a ripple in the air itself. A rift in reality.

The Way was taking physical form right before his eyes. His mental bridge was becoming real. He had found the key.

He stared at it, barely comprehending, aware of the surging forces all around him.

'Go on, Matt! Go *on*!'

He looked across at Vince, who was backing away up the stairs. He looked frightened. He looked exhilarated. 'Go *on*!'

Matt took a step forward, then another.

Suddenly the shimmering disc rushed around him, engulfing him. Swallowing him. He felt an intense dizziness, the gorge rising in his throat.

He closed his eyes, and a sudden darkness stole over him. He blacked out.

13

TRAPPED

He was alone. He had never felt more alone than this.

And yet . . .

He was looking down on himself from a distance, it seemed. Watching himself: a figure adrift in nothingness.

All around was impenetrable darkness. A darkness so deep it was almost a physical thing, a solid. Black stone, engulfing everything.

He rubbed at his face, and he saw the figure of himself reach up and rub at its eyes. It was like looking in a distant mirror. Watching an image of himself. He remembered Gramps' words: *battling inside our heads is a whole set of alternative selves – the people we might have been*. That was the basis of Alternity: the realm of alternatives, the world inhabited by our rejected selves, our darker sides.

He turned – somehow he turned, although he realized he had no real sense of his own body. There was another figure, another Matt. Turning, peering around, looking lost.

He closed his eyes and the darkness was complete. What had he done? What had Vince led him into?

Did all these versions of himself feel this way, he wondered. Were they all as lost and confused, as vulnerable and scared, as he was?

In that case, *which one was he*? Where was he? Who was he?

He felt as if he was sinking, submerging in the madness of repeated, unanswerable questions. Sucked down by forces too awesome for him to comprehend: a leaf dragged from its tree by an October gale, a fish caught up in a tidal wave.

He was in Mad City. Loonyville. Gagaland.

He'd been taken by the family madness, and Vince had led him right up to its front door and helped him ring the bell.

He was in a passageway, the maze of his dreams. Brick walls rose up on either side of him, their surfaces smoothed by the ages, slick with a slimy moisture that seemed to seep out through the mortar.

He felt cold, and his lungs were filled with the foul, foetid odour of decay. He hugged himself and struggled to control his ragged breathing, to cut off a self-pitying whimper – because once it started, he knew he would lose control altogether.

He looked down at the stained concrete floor. A shallow channel ran along the centre. It glistened wetly with moisture from the walls. There was a red tinge to the moisture, he saw. The red of blood.

He became aware of something approaching. There were no sounds, he could see nothing, but he knew there was something there. It was a presence rising up in his mind, a dark shape which he knew would materialize at any moment.

He looked both ways, but they appeared to be identical: a short length of corridor, then a blank wall as the route turned left or right.

Which way?

He chose at random and ran until he came to a junction. Was this the right direction? He didn't know, he could only hope.

He plunged on into the gloom.

He had been running for what seemed like forever. Along endless brick-walled corridors, coming to junctions and guessing which way to go. He had no idea of direction, only that he had to keep going.

The presence was always there – sometimes near, sometimes distant. Occasionally he heard sounds, but he could never be sure what they were or where they came from. They might even have been his own sounds echoing back to him, for all he knew.

He had started talking to himself, chivvying himself along. 'Left or right? Forward or back?'

Left.

Left again.

You're going in circles. You don't want to go in circles: you might just catch up with yourself.

But *was* he talking to himself, he suddenly

wondered. Telling himself to keep going, or to go back. Telling himself that he had to run for his life, or that he should turn and confront whatever it was that was pursuing him.

Voices in his head.

Battling inside our heads is a whole set of alternative selves ... That was where Gramps had claimed Alternity came from: all the alternative versions of ourselves, battling it out in our heads, forging an alternative reality that haunts our dreams. The voices in our heads.

But he was *in* Alternity! If such voices came from Alternity, then were there other, deeper Alternities hidden within this one: an endless sequence of Russian dolls, one inside the other?

He felt dizzy, just at the thought. Like when he had come round first of all, and had seen all those alternative versions of himself – losing track of his own identity in an infinite hall of mirrors.

He shook himself, made himself keep running. 'Come on, boy,' he muttered. 'Gotta keep going. Gotta keep on.'

But eventually it was no good, he had to stop. He had been running forever, and his legs were like concrete.

He had to stop.

He came to a corner. It seemed darker here, welcoming.

He slumped against the wall, slid down. He was unconscious before he even reached the floor.

*

He could hear gulls mewing in the distance. People laughing. He could smell the fresh, briny smell of the sea.

He opened his eyes, saw sand and shingle in close-up. He was lying, face down, on the beach.

Had he escaped? Had he broken free from Alternity? He tried to think what it was that he had done that might have been the key to his escape. He had run until his legs would carry him no further. Was it simply that he had recognized that running would get him nowhere, that he could stop fleeing and stay in one place?

He should have known it would never be as simple as that.

He turned on to his side and, gradually, his eyes focused on a pale object, a little way away from his face.

Embedded in the beach was a human skull.

A jagged crack ran upwards from its left eye-socket, and crawling all over the thing were hundreds of those small brown sand-flies that rise up in clouds from dried seaweed along the tide-line.

Horrified, he looked more closely at the sand and shingle: scattered everywhere were small white fragments of bone, broken vertebrae, lost teeth.

Slowly, he swung his gaze out to sea. Dark storm clouds hung over deep red waves. It was the sea of his dreams, the sea of blood. Debris floated in the bay, dismembered body-parts – hands, legs, torsos, heads even – and flocks of gulls soared and swooped, feasting on the carnage, their white plumage stained a gruesome, sticky crimson.

He twisted away and threw up on the beach.

He struggled to control his breathing, he had to calm down. For this was no longer a dream, he was actually *here* . . .

Acrid traces of vomit burned at the back of his throat and nose with every breath.

He made himself look around again. He had to get out of here, but how do you wake yourself from a dream that has entirely swallowed you up?

For a few seconds he watched the figure of an old derelict – a man of sixty or more, wrapped up in numerous layers of filthy brown rags – shuffling along the tideline, turning over the jetsam with the open toe of one of his boots. Matt wondered what he was hoping to find.

His senses were growing numb to all the horrors he was seeing, he realized. Even when the tramp squatted to pick something out of a dark, tangled mass, Matt didn't look away. Even when the tramp raised his trophy to his mouth and bit into it.

Only when the old man wiped his mouth with one foul sleeve and turned to stare at him did Matt rise and turn away. The man's eyes were deeply bloodshot, and there was an intense humanity about his look that reached out to Matt, breaking through his barriers.

Matt climbed the concrete steps to the Promenade and was surprised to see how many holidaymakers were here, despite the deep gloom of the weather.

He stopped himself, suddenly frightened at how easy it was to accept this grim distortion as reality: a world of holidays and football and school and work, a world where nothing was really any different.

The people were dressed in a strange assortment of clothing, as if they had all taken part in a lucky dip at some monstrous jumble sale. Striped blazers, frilly summer frocks with parasols, mismatched items of school uniform, pin-striped trousers with torn T-shirts, patchwork waistcoats, wide-brimmed straw hats, long leather coats, high boots, fur caps.

Couples strolled, arm in arm, their faces pale and hollowed out, as if they were being eaten away from within. Emaciated dogs tottered along after grotesquely overweight owners. Tiny children, covered only in dark red 'mud' from the beach, chased one another through the crowds, while yet others gathered round an ice-cream vendor's stall.

And all the time, as Matt walked along the Prom, eyes followed him, tracking his progress. Even the children stopped what they were doing to stare.

He made for one of the paths that led up the grass slope towards Bay Road, grateful to be leaving the crowds behind.

At the top, he looked back down the cliff: hundreds of pale faces were tipped up towards him; beyond them, the deep red bay spread out towards the horizon.

Occasional cars steered crooked courses along the road, their grim-faced drivers leaning forward to stare at the road ahead, gripping the steering wheel with white-knuckled intensity.

He walked along to where the road forked, then crossed over to the white stone memorial. He would have walked straight past, but something made him pause. He looked more closely at the memorial: on each of its six sides there should have been a list of names of the town's men lost in the wars, but there were none, just a blank white panel.

He hurried on. He didn't understand why, but something about those missing names chilled him deeply.

The house looked the same as ever: tall, slightly dishevelled, the small patch of front garden looking neat and ordered as a result of the girls' attention.

Vince's car was up on blocks in the parking bay, and thin legs poked out from underneath.

'Vince?' Matt said cautiously. He swallowed, and added, 'What are you doing, Vince? Why did you make me come here? How do I get out?'

The legs twisted, and a body rolled out from under the car. Vince propped himself up on one elbow and stared up at Matt, his white face smeared with oil. Only . . .

His eyes were reddened and his lips were dry and cracked. His hair hung in black, greasy strands.

He opened his mouth and a half-strangled croak emerged.

He started to get to his feet, and Matt backed away. This wasn't Vince: it was a cruel distortion of him. And it was holding a long-bladed screwdriver – gripping it as if it were a dagger.

With a strangled wail, the Vince-creature lurched towards him.

Matt darted into the house.

It took a few seconds for his eyes to adjust to the gloom. Nothing looked different. He peered out through the distorted glass of the front door. As far as he could see, Vince had returned to his car. He started to calm down. He had to think his situation through. He had to work out how to get out of here. There had to be a way!

The alternative was too awful to consider.

The living-room door was ajar, and Matt suddenly became aware of a sound: the revving of car engines. Kirsty was playing her motor racing game.

He pushed the door open and saw her small head over the sofa. He entered the room and sat at the end of the sofa. She didn't even look up, she was too intent on the game.

She didn't look any different from normal.

'Kirsty,' he said. 'We have to talk again. I have to get out of here.'

She ignored him.

Eventually, the race ended and she glanced sideways at him then. 'Poor cousin Matthew,' she said. 'You should never have trusted Vince. Tina doesn't trust him. She says he's not nice.'

'How do I get out of here?'

She looked confused. He had to remind himself that she was only seven.

'Out of this place,' he explained. 'How do I get back to the real world?'

She shook her head. 'This seems very real to *me*,' she said uncertainly. 'Tina said you were strange – I think I understand why now.'

He went through to the kitchen, but it was empty. A hover mower whined nasally from the back garden. He went across to the window.

It was a peaceful summer scene. Uncle Mike was mowing a patch of the lawn, over and over again, as if he was stuck in a private time warp. Carol was clipping a hedge into a rippling, distorted shape that Matt didn't quite recognize and wasn't sure that he *wanted* to recognize.

He pushed the back door open and stepped outside, suddenly aware of the eyes turning to him.

'I . . .' He stopped, unsure what he had been about to say.

Carol smiled, which was not particularly reassuring. 'Matthew,' she said. 'How nice to see you. Look, Mike, Tina: we have a visitor.'

Tina? He hadn't seen Tina.

He started to turn, then stopped. She was coming round the corner of the house, carrying a hosepipe.

She smiled then raised the hose. With a deft twist of her hand, she turned the hose on and directed it at Matt.

A bright red spray emerged, covering him in an instant.

He gasped and turned away, but his mouth was full of the sharp taste of blood.

He stumbled and fell – he had forgotten that there was a step down to the lawn.

On his knees, he looked up. He raised his hands in front of his face as Tina advanced with the hose.

Too late, he became aware of the insistent clack-clack-clack of Carol's hedge shears approaching. She lunged at him, and he felt cold, hard steel striking the back of his head.

He tumbled away, rolling, twisting, trying to get his bearings.

When he finally stopped moving, he found himself lying on his back. He looked up, and all he could see was a dark silhouette against the sky, and then the whirring blades as his uncle's mower descended.

Intense, metal taste of blood. A booming pain filling his body. He was alive.

Had he found the way out?

He opened his eyes. He was lying on the beach again, further down, where the sand was packed hard, stained a dark, wet pink by the bloody surf.

Suddenly he understood the meaning of the memorial, the missing lists of names. What did death mean in this place? Nothing.

He pushed himself to his knees and peered around. Nothing had changed. Nothing ever changed.

The old tramp was a short distance away. Watching him. Smiling softly. This close, he looked older than he had before.

'You're looking lost, boy,' said the tramp. 'You don't want to be looking lost here, boy. You don't want to be losing your grip.'

Matt stared at him. This was the voice that had filled his head earlier, when he had been struggling through the brick-walled maze . . . *guiding* him.

'You?' he said. 'Gramps, is that really you?'

The tramp chuckled. In a single movement, he turned and dropped to the beach so that he was sitting, watching Matt. He shook his head, still smiling.

Matt went on: 'But you're one of us, aren't you? A Wareden.' From an earlier generation: a guardian of the Way.

The tramp was still shaking his head. Finally he said, 'Don't you see, boy? I'm *you*. Every time you dream of this place you leave a part of yourself behind. I'm you, boy. I'm you when you've been here long enough to realize there's no way out, that this is all there is. I'm just an old tramp, boy, and this is my home.'

Matt stared at him in horror, unable to believe, unable not to believe. 'You mean . . . You mean, there's really no way out of here? No escape from Alternity?'

The tramp shook his head, sadness in his eyes. 'Nobody gets out of here,' he said. 'If there was a way out, then Alternity would spill over into the real world, swamping it, destroying it. And you know what happens when it spills out, don't you, boy? Eh?'

Matt thought. 'The graves,' he said slowly. 'The vicar described it as "a madness", "a night of horrific violence": 1898 – it must have broken out then.'

The tramp nodded. 'All it takes is a moment of weakness, a bridge between the two realms. All the time Alternity is reaching out to people out there: people who might cause the Way to be opened. And then it bursts out, boy – the power, the madness. Just think about it: all the trapped, tormented souls in Alternity bursting out. They take over the living and use their bodies to their own twisted ends.

'But there are too many, boy. *Far too many* escaping souls – all breaking out, all fighting with each other to possess the living . . . they drive people out of their own heads.'

'Is that what happened? In 1898? I've seen the graves, the six families . . .'

'Possessed by Alternity, or killed by those who were possessed. Thank God it was stopped in time.'

'How?'

'The Way. Your great-grandfather didn't really understand his responsibilities. He didn't understand the dangers and he experimented . . . He opened the Way and Alternity spilled out. He *invited* it, I think. At first, anyway. He wrote in his diary that he thought it was a force for good. He came to his senses quickly and he managed to close the Way. With the bridge between the two realms closed, the madness dissipated and the dark powers weakened. Six families – it could easily have been more.'

He spread his hands and gestured at the warped world around them. 'All this,' he went on. 'All this is made out of all that is foul and corrupt in human nature. You've seen only a tiny fraction of it: multiply that by a thousand, a million, and you still wouldn't be able to grasp how much evil our kind is capable of. And just you think what it would be like if this vile power was set loose in your reality . . .' The tramp was staring at Matt, a twisted, bitter smile on his face. 'A madness indeed – but really it's far *more* than a madness. It's violent and evil, a force that destroys everything in its path. Give it a chance and it will spread out from the ruptured Way like a dark cancer across the countryside.'

He leant forward now, his knuckles pressing into the reddened sand. 'There's no way out, boy. We're sealed in here, good and proper, and that's the way it should be. No, the real art for us is to *stay* here . . .'

'What do you mean?'

'This isn't really Alternity,' said the tramp. 'This is Alternity's dream of itself – a kind of limbo, an in-between world built up from your own mind and from the minds of everyone who dreams of this place. Alternity itself is a realm of pure energy, seething forces and powers that are impossible for us to conceive of – we just don't have the language, or the concepts. It's a welter of primeval forces, where there's no "you" any more. It's the chaos from which the universe was formed. And it's the chaos into which the world will ultimately return if it is ever allowed to seep out.

'If you lose a grip on this limbo dreamworld, then all that remains is Alternity. That's your choice, boy: this macabre dream, or annihilation in Alternity. They're all you have left.'

Matt was shaking his head. He couldn't believe there was no way back. He couldn't believe that this was it.

The tramp was watching him closely. 'You'll believe it,' he told Matt. 'One day, you'll come round on the beach and you'll believe it. Just like me!' He gave a short, loud laugh, then heaved himself to his feet and resumed his gruesome search along the tideline.

He had an idea: a single sliver of hope to cling on to. It was all he had.

It was about eight kilometres to Crooked Elms, but he had nothing better to do with what passed for time in this perverted realm. He walked at a steady pace, concentrating hard to make sure he was on the right road.

Eventually he came to the roundabout on the edge of town. He stepped into the road, determined not to look too closely at what the crows were picking at in the gutter.

There was a sudden brain-shaking blast of a horn – he looked up and instantly threw himself back on to the verge. The gust of air from the passing lorry spun him like a windmill's sail, and he sprawled in the dirt. He watched as the lorry mounted the roundabout and went straight across, leaving twin tracks of ploughed-up dirt in its wake.

Moments later, the lorry was gone.

He cursed himself. He had to pay attention. *Concentrate*.

Gathering his breath, he looked carefully before crossing. For the rest of his long walk, he clambered up the verge at the first sound of traffic. He was too tired to make this walk again, he knew.

Copperas Wood formed a dark fringe on the edge of the field to his right. Not far to go now.

He kept walking until he came to a gate at the end of a rough track. He could go down here and cut through the woods, he knew. It would bring him out into the field behind Gramps' paddock.

He looked at the dark shadows under the trees.

He shook his head and turned away. He would take his chances with the road.

A short time later, he was passing the first houses of Crooked Elms. Pale faces crowded together at every window, staring out, following his progress. Clawed hands scraped at the glass in frustration, longing.

They wanted him. He knew that at any second they might rush out at him and he forced himself not to think what they might do. Forced himself not to think of Uncle Mike's lawnmower descending on him . . .

But why were they waiting?

He quickened his pace.

He reached the crossroads and turned right. Seconds later, he was walking into the semicircular driveway.

He looked up at the house, puzzled.

It didn't feel right. Something was missing.

He went up to the front door. It was locked. He peered inside: everything looked familiar, but somehow it was *different*.

He followed the path around the side of the house until he came to the back door. He took a brick and smashed a pane of glass, then reached in, groped around until he found the key and then unlocked the door.

He went straight to the basement. He knew what was missing now: his grandparents' house felt just like anywhere else. There was nothing special about it. The place was dead.

The basement. A long, low-ceilinged room, lit by a single, bare light-bulb. He didn't feel dizzy, he didn't feel as if consciousness would slip away at any moment. His feet didn't drag, didn't feel as if they were encased in concrete.

'Never the doors of the righteous be breached.
The minds of the pure are our shield,
Protect us from evil, protect us from fear,
Shine light where the shadow concealed.'

It wasn't going to work. He tried again. He tried shuffling the words, but where before it was as if the poem had rearranged *itself*, now it stubbornly refused to find a new form.

149

The magic had gone. This Way was dead in Alternity.

His only hope had let him down.

He sank to the floor in desolation.

Now he knew why the villagers had let him pass: no need to hurry, since he was going nowhere.

He was trapped. He really was trapped.

14

THE BRIDGE

The headstones crowded together in silent ranks. A motley assortment of older, lichen-encrusted slabs, tilted and smoothed with age, were interspersed with a few clean, sharp-edged, marble headstones.

All of them were blank, like the war memorial that stood above the bay at Bathside. Some of the graves were marked with shrivelled, decaying flowers. Others were bare, the earth around them disturbed, as if animals had been digging.

The wrought-iron fence enclosing the dead families from 1898 was caked with rust.

Matt went closer.

Not rust, he saw: it was a deeper red, the red of dried blood. The stones within were bare, just like all the others.

Just then Matt heard a scratching sound, a scraping: fingernails on stone. One of the six slabs started to move, vibrating as some unseen force wrestled with it from below.

Matt backed away and the movement subsided, the scraping sounds ceased.

He tugged the heavy church door by its iron-ring

handle. Inside, the church offered cool refuge from the muggy, stormy heat of the day. He slid into a pew and closed his eyes. He had to think, he had to get things straight in his mind.

The family talent: it was a special sensitivity, an ability to form a mental bridge between the two realms. But he had been completely swallowed up by Alternity! How could he hope to form such a link when he was wholly trapped in one of the realms? He had nowhere to form a bridge to . . . He was just an ordinary person. Trapped.

No wonder the house had lost its special atmosphere: he was not sensitive to the Way from this side.

He remembered the tramp's words: *Nobody gets out of here . . . this is all there is.*

He heard a sound from the far end of the church. There was somebody down there. Hiding? Spying on him? He remembered all the staring faces behind the windows in the village's houses. Had they come after him?

It was the vicar: the one Carol had called David, the one who had waited for Matt in the hospital garden with tales of madness and the Devil.

The man gave a slight start when he saw Matt sitting in the church. Then he walked along the central aisle towards him. He smiled. 'We don't have many visitors these days,' he said. 'Faith is such a rare thing here. Even the young don't swallow our tall stories any more.'

Matt stared at him. And then, slowly, he started to smile.

The vicar raised his eyebrows, clearly confused by Matt's expression.

Matt stood up quickly and turned towards the door. 'Sorry,' he said. 'I've got to go.'

'I wouldn't if I were you,' said the vicar. 'They're waiting outside. You're new here, aren't you? They don't like your sort, you see. They hate you. They associate you with all that they've lost. They want nothing more than to get out of this damnable place, yet you and your kind keep them here. You keep them trapped.' The vicar's voice was becoming steadily shriller. 'You can wait here. Really, you can wait here. Stay with me – go on, you'll be much better off with me!'

And then Matt saw that he was carrying something small, something that glinted in the dim light of the church's interior. A knife of some sort.

Matt ran to the door and pushed it open.

They were waiting in the churchyard: ghoulish faces all turned towards the door, waiting for Matt to emerge. Old ladies with broken bottles in their hands, children with hammers or sticks, a large black dog straining at its leash. A young mother, clutching a baby to her bare breast, held a machete in her free hand.

Matt darted among jostling headstones and found the small path that led around to the back of the church.

He came to a high stone wall, a row of plaques at its foot – these still bore names, he saw, and then he remembered: the cremated. *Ashes*, Gramps had said. *There's no way back from ashes*.

Why wasn't the crowd following, he wondered suddenly. What were they waiting for?

And then he heard the scratching again. And he felt the vibrations in the ground beneath his feet. He was standing by a small, plain headstone and now he could see the ground bulging upwards.

He backed away.

There was an abrupt tearing sound and the ground burst open. A figure pushed its way free of the loose soil.

A man.

Halfway out of the ground, he stopped and brushed soil from his face.

The man was young, dressed in black. He had a white collar around his neck. He was a vicar!

Back when Gramps had been young there had been a vicar: a strong man. An evil man. Gramps had defeated him – had he been trapped in Alternity as punishment?

Was this man the Reverend Harold Allbright?

The man looked at Matt and smiled crookedly. 'Ah,' he said in a rich, deep voice. 'How *nice*: a Wareden. It's been *such* a long wait.'

As he started to pull himself free of the ground, Matt turned and ran.

At the front of the church they were still waiting.

He had nowhere to turn to. He stepped out into a

pool of sunlight that had suddenly broken through the clouds.

He recounted the first vicar's words in his mind – *even the young* – determined to lodge them there. He had to hold on to that thought. No matter what they did to him.

The dog got to him first. It broke free from its owner and came bounding towards Matt, its teeth bared, drooling white foam. He felt those hard white teeth closing on his throat as he fell back towards the church, and then he felt nothing at all.

He could hear gulls mewing in the distance. People laughing. He could smell the fresh, briny smell of the sea.

He opened his eyes, saw sand and shingle in front of his face. He was lying on the beach.

He knew better now than to hope he had escaped. He raised a hand to his neck, suddenly remembering the dog's attack.

The tramp was a short distance away, watching him, chuckling. 'Believe me yet?'

He ignored the tramp, climbed to his feet and brushed the sand from his clothes. He knew what he had to do. He hurried up to the Promenade. As before, everybody stopped and stared at him. He tried to ignore them.

He paused at the memorial. He had to work out how he was going to do this. Death might have lost meaning here, but pain had not. Instinctively, he reached for his throat again, and thought of that dog.

Vince was still working on his car. He had an aerosol can and a rag and he kept spraying a small patch on the driver's door then rubbing it vigorously with his rag. Spraying and rubbing, spraying and rubbing.

But his eyes weren't on his work, they were continually flitting from side to side, watching. Waiting.

Matt backed away. He could play the waiting game, too.

Time didn't seem to be passing. The sun stayed high in the sky, hidden most of the time behind the heavy blanket of clouds. And Vince remained at the front of the house. Matt waited, a short distance up an alleyway, as far out of sight as he could manage. Every so often he emerged and peered along the street to make sure that Vince was still there.

What if Vince never moved from that spot? It was a possibility he had to consider.

He went deeper into the alleyway. He knew there wasn't a back way into his aunt's garden, but what if . . .?

The alleyway was enclosed by high, rendered walls and cluttered at regular intervals by green wheelybins. A number of tall wooden doors were set into the wall. He approached the last of these, pushed it open, and passed through into an overgrown garden. He looked around, but nobody seemed to be aware of him; there were no staring faces at the windows.

He crossed the garden and clambered over a

wooden fence. He tried to recall the view from the box-room window so that he could work out where he was.

He headed across the garden, ignoring the sudden gasp of surprise from an elderly man who had been spraying his roses. Matt pulled himself up on to the next high wall and was relieved to see that the garden was empty. He noticed the small patch of short grass where Mike had been mowing, and he shuddered in sudden recollection.

He swung himself over the wall and landed in a crouch in a large patch of summer bedding.

At the back door he paused.

The kitchen was empty. He went inside.

There was a sound coming from the dining room, so he hurried through into the hallway before he was noticed. He could hear the sound of a computer game from the living room.

He stepped across to the door and peered inside. A single head was just visible over the sofa: Kirsty. He took a deep breath and stepped into the room, shutting the door gently behind him and leaning on it.

'Cousin Matthew!'

He turned. Tina was standing in the corner by a bookshelf. Smiling.

Kirsty looked up from where she was sitting on the floor. She glanced from her sister to Matt and back again, looking puzzled, a little frightened. 'Tina?' she said. 'Why are you looking at Matt like that?'

Matt backed away from the older girl.

She was coming towards him, still smiling. She didn't have any weapons – but then, Matt realized grimly, she didn't look as if she needed any. She looked as if she was preparing to tear him limb from limb . . .

And slowly.

Matt raised his arms, trying to prepare himself for another attack.

Just then a large vase smashed over Tina's head.

For an instant it looked as if the older girl would not react. She blinked, straightened a little, blinked again. And then she slumped to the floor, blood seeping through her straight brown hair.

Matt stared aghast at Kirsty, who was now standing on the sofa, wiping her hands down her front. She looked apologetic.

She glanced at Matt, then looked away. In a very quiet voice she said, 'I hate it when she gets like that. She knows I hate it.'

She straightened up, then stepped down from the sofa. In a stronger voice, she said, 'She'll be back, though. She never leaves me alone for long.'

Matt made himself think. He had to stay in control. 'Kirsty,' he said. 'I need your help. I'm trapped here. I can't get out.'

She looked puzzled.

'The bridge, Kirsty! You can make the bridge in your mind.' He stepped towards her and placed a hand gently on her arm to try to reassure her. 'Kirsty, please. Remember the poems that Gramps taught us – the ones that close the doors in our minds. You can use them to open doors, too. I need you to open a door for me, Kirsty, to let me back through. You're still out there in the real world, Kirsty – it's just a part of you that's here with me. You can still form that bridge.'

She still looked confused, frightened by his intensity.

'Never the doors of the righteous be breached,' he recited at her. 'Go on. Please, Kirsty: say the words.'

Hesitantly, she recited the poem for him. Immediately, he felt the words' calming influence spreading, a bond forging itself between Kirsty and himself.

A dark shadow fell across the window.

Vince.

'The words have the power, Kirsty,' Matt pleaded. 'Use them to open the door. Swap them around, reverse them. Just keep saying them!'

The window burst inwards and a bloody fist tangled in the net curtains.

Kirsty gasped and turned to the window.

'Please, Kirsty.'

'Never the shield of our minds be breached, shine shadow, where light had concealed,' she said. 'Protect us from evil, protect us from fear.' Once she had started, the words came cascading out.

They repeated the last line together: 'Shine shadow, where light had concealed!' Immediately, Kirsty started to repeat the distorted poem, mixing its words up even further.

There was a grunt from beyond the shattered

window. Vince was staring curiously at his bloodied fist. Then he wiped it down his front and started to clamber into the room.

And, suddenly, the air shifted and an intense heat descended.

'Go *on*!' Matt cried at his chanting cousin.

A disc formed, hanging in the air about two metres in front of Kirsty.

Matt lunged towards it and suddenly the shimmering disc folded itself around him, engulfing him. An intense dizziness washed over him and he fell forward on to his knees, struggling to remain conscious.

PART FOUR
THE RECKONING

15

MISSING

His body was aching, his limbs felt heavy. It was as if a great weight was pressing him down into the hard floor, making every breath a gargantuan effort.

His eyes started to adjust to the darkness: an irregular assortment of shapes all around him, a horizontal line of light somewhere above him. The air smelt musty, unused.

He was in the basement of his grandparents' house. He should have known that this was where he would reappear – he had foolishly expected to emerge in his aunt's house at Bathside, but the Way was here.

He felt consciousness starting to seep away.

'Never the doors of the righteous be breached,' he gasped, gaining strength with every word. 'The minds of the pure are our shield.'

He forced himself into a sitting position. The dark shapes he could see were the stacked boxes and bags, the horizontal line was the light seeping under the door at the top of the basement stairs.

'Protect us from evil, protect us from fear,
Shine light where the shadow concealed.'

He stood up and staggered towards the stairs and climbed them on all fours.

At the top, he stood again, dragged the door open and toppled out into the hallway, savouring the sudden bright sunlight.

He was alone in the house, he felt certain. Vince must have left him – perhaps he had even fled in panic at the sight of the Way opening up and Matt being engulfed.

He wasn't sorry to be alone. He felt weak and confused. He needed to gather himself, to work out what had happened. But in a strange way, he realized, he felt strong, too. He had confronted Alternity and mastered it, he had learnt to control the family talent.

Was that really why Vince had pushed him into going through with it? To help him confront and master this thing? Perhaps it was just the morbid curiosity of the outsider. In a way Vince was very much like Tina – an ungifted, ordinary individual on the edges of something special. Perhaps he had simply wanted to see what would happen.

But Matt remembered his grandfather's and the tramp's warnings about how Alternity could reach out to weak minds and use them to try to open the Way . . . Was that why Vince was so drawn to this place? Was he a mere puppet, controlled by dark forces?

Matt went through to the kitchen and tried the taps, but the water had been turned off. He glanced at the back door and was momentarily surprised to see that the glass was not broken . . . but that had been in Alternity . . .

He shuddered, then rubbed at his face. He had to get a grip on himself.

He found some tonic water in a cupboard and drank deeply, ignoring the bitter aftertaste. He took the key from its shelf just inside the back door and let himself out. The side of the house was in shadow, and for a moment his brain didn't recognize the slumped shape at the foot of the wall.

A body.

It was a man's body.

Matt stepped back into the kitchen doorway.

It was the young vicar. His face was covered in dried blood . . . his big glasses lay a short distance away, smashed.

Had Matt failed to break free, after all? Was this still the gruesome half-world between reality and Alternity? He remembered the crowd of villagers lining up in the churchyard, armed with assorted sticks, machetes, broken bottles. Had they turned on the young vicar, once they had despatched Matt?

He tried to calm down, to think things through in a rational way. He thought of the Way Kirsty had opened up for him: passing through it had been identical to the first time he had passed through the Way, so why would it merely return him to

Alternity? He looked at the intact glass in the back door, then outside at the high blue sky.

He shook his head.

This wasn't Alternity. It didn't *feel* like Alternity.

He stepped outside again and approached the vicar.

He was breathing! He was alive!

Matt crouched down and pulled at the man's dog collar, trying to loosen it.

In response to his touch, the vicar flinched weakly, then opened his eyes.

Matt jerked away, convinced the eyes would be red and staring, but they were grey, watery, unfocused.

The vicar opened his mouth a crack. 'I . . . I need help,' he croaked. 'It . . . hurts.'

'OK,' said Matt. 'I'll get help.'

The vicar seized his wrist, stopping Matt from rising. 'I . . . felt something,' he said. 'Something here. Stan Wareden asked me to watch over his house, so I came. I *felt* something. Calling to me. The Devil was calling to me . . . I tried to resist . . . but I had to come . . . so weak . . .'

Matt worked his way free, disturbed by the vicar's words. Had the vicar really detected something happening with the Way? Had Matt's exploits had some wider effect? He remembered the warnings about the dangers posed by any seepage through the Way . . . the graves in the churchyard. Had his activities weakened the Way somehow? Had Alternity been reaching out through a weakness he had forged?

He went inside and lifted the telephone from its cradle, half expecting the line to be dead. The dialling tone hummed in his ear and he keyed 999. 'Ambulance, please,' he said. 'I need an ambulance.'

'We've been looking for you. You've caused us a lot of trouble. Your mum's been worried sick.'

The man had introduced himself as Detective Sergeant Cooper. He was a dark-haired man with a moustache, and he was wearing a suit that didn't quite fit the broad shape of his body.

Matt leant back against the door-frame. He was exhausted. He'd been to his own private hell and back. And now he was being told off by a policeman who didn't have the faintest idea what really went on in this village, this house.

Out in the drive, Sergeant Cooper's colleague watched as the paramedics eased the vicar into the ambulance. Cooper had parked his car in the road.

'You could at least have called her to say you were all right.'

Matt didn't understand. 'What day is it?' he asked.

Cooper looked at him strangely. 'Wednesday,' he said. 'The 20th.'

Matt stared at him. 'I . . . I lost track,' he said. He had been missing for a whole week.

'You just found him, you say.'

Matt nodded. He had to think quickly. He took the back-door key from his pocket and held it out for the policeman to see. 'I had a key,' he said.

'I knew this place was empty. I didn't know there'd be a fuss.'

'What about the Reverend Walters?'

Matt struggled to come up with an explanation. 'I'd just got up. I came down here and found him.'

'"Just got up"? It's half past three in the afternoon.'

'Like I say,' said Matt. 'I lost track.'

The ambulance pulled away and the other policeman approached them. 'Unconscious,' he said, glancing at Matt. 'He's taken one hell of a beating.'

Cooper took Matt by the arm. 'Come on,' he said. 'We're going to need a statement.'

'Where the hell have you been?'

What a lovely welcome home, Matt thought. He'd been attacked by lawn mowers, zombie vicars and mad dogs, he'd found another vicar half-beaten to death, he'd been quizzed by the police and now this: his angry mother laying into him in a police interview room.

'Gramps' house,' he said. 'I couldn't help it. I had to think.'

She was shaking her head. 'Oh no,' she said. 'Don't think we didn't look there. Where have you been?'

He moved towards the door. 'You wouldn't want to know,' he said. She was wearing the suit she had bought for her interviews. 'Shouldn't you be working?' he asked.

'Of course I should damned well be working!' she

168

screeched at him. 'But I got a phone call from the police, didn't I? They told me my son, who's been missing for a week, has turned up at my father's house along with someone who's been beaten nearly to death. So I thought that, on the whole, the best thing to do would be to come down here to the police station and drag you out of whatever hole you've dug for yourself, didn't I?'

He walked out into the corridor. How could he even begin to explain?

16
CATCHING UP

The police station was down in old Bathside, near the docks at Eastquay. They walked back towards Aunt Carol's house by the bay.

Matt's mother kept up a brisk, angry pace. The sound of her heels clicking loudly as she walked only served to emphasize the silence between the two of them.

'How's work?' Matt asked eventually.

He thought she wasn't going to answer, then finally she said, 'It was fine until today. I'm temping at a printing company now. I started yesterday, despite everything. It took my mind off things, at least. I don't know if they'll have me back after this, though.'

More silence.

They passed the park, then turned left down Bagshaw Terrace. Matt looked warily at the rows of windows, half expecting to see ghoulish faces pressed against the glass, watching him. Waiting.

But they were just windows. Ordinary windows.

The bay came into sight, up ahead. Grey-blue, no

sign of anything floating, no crimson-stained gulls scavenging in the waves.

He might have mastered the family talent, he realized, but now he had to come to terms with everyday reality: everything he saw disturbed him, as if at any moment he might be dumped back into that gruesome other world. He trusted nothing.

'How's Gramps?' he asked. Seven days. Such a lot could have happened in seven days.

His mother glanced at him. 'You'll have to visit him this evening,' she said. 'I've called him already, but he wants to see you. He's been worried sick about you. I didn't tell him you'd gone, I didn't want to upset him, but Tina blurted it out before I could warn her.'

Still in hospital? 'I didn't think he'd still be there,' he said.

His mother glanced at him. 'He had an infection,' she told him. 'It often happens when old people go into hospital. The infection brought on a bout of pneumonia. He's pulling through, though. If everything goes well, he should be out in a few days.'

They passed the war memorial – columns of names etched into each of its six sides – and, just before turning into Carol's street, Matt's mother paused. 'Matt,' she said, hesitantly. 'Your father came down on Sunday. He was worried sick. We all were.'

'And?'

She shook her head. 'And nothing, Matt. He

came down to see if he could help. We had an argument. He blamed me because he thought I should have kept more control over you. I blamed him because I was sure you were trying to make your way back to Norwich to see him.' She smiled. 'It was just like old times.'

For an instant, he thought she meant . . . but then she shook her head. 'No, Matt. There's no going back. But eventually we agreed that we both want what's best for you. Your father agreed to pay the deposit if I can find somewhere to live, then we'll come to whatever arrangement suits you best. You're old enough to work out what's right.

'And, Matt, you really should have talked. You shouldn't have just gone off like that.'

He turned away. He couldn't explain. Not now, perhaps not ever. It would only make things worse.

They were all there, waiting. As soon as the door shut behind Matt and his mother, they crowded round – Carol, Mike and the girls in the kitchen and living-room doorways, Vince at the top of the stairs – all of them staring.

Matt smiled. 'Hi,' he said brightly. 'Missed me?'

Tina turned away angrily, pulling her sister back into the living room. Mike stood, shaking his head in disapproval, while Carol forged her stiff smile across her features before saying, 'Matthew. We were concerned.'

Vince stood nonchalantly at the top of the stairs. He was watching Matt closely, and he was smiling.

Matt met his eyes briefly, then followed his mother through to the kitchen.

Carol was slicing carrots on a marble cutting-board. Matt glanced out of the window into the garden, recalling how good she was with the shears . . . He was going to have to learn how to separate his memories – the real and the alternative – and quickly. He would go mad otherwise – he felt sure of that.

His presence made Carol uneasy, he could see. She didn't know how to handle him, she didn't know what to say.

'Did Dad stay for long?' he asked. He knew Carol didn't like his father. Merely referring to his visit made her visibly tense.

'A couple of hours,' his mother said quickly. 'Long enough.'

Long enough to argue. Long enough to negotiate over his future. Long enough to know they had no future themselves.

'Call him,' she went on. 'Ask him yourself. I'm sure he's waiting by the phone.'

'Good day at work?' Carol asked cheerfully.

'I had to leave early,' his mother said in a tightly controlled voice.

Matt left them to it. From the hallway, he peered through the open door into the living room. They were all in there, just an ordinary family.

He went upstairs. There was a telephone on the first-floor landing. He took it from the top of a chest of drawers and sat on the floor. After a few seconds,

he picked up the receiver and listened for the dialling tone to make sure no one was using the other
extension. Then he dialled his home number.

'Hi, Nigel Guilder here, all your copying and
reprographic requirements satisfied with the minimum of fuss. Afraid I can't make it to the phone
right now, but if you'd be so good as to leave your
number after the tone I'll get back to you at the first
opportunity. Thanks for calling.'

He listened to the tone. He thought about saying
something, but decided against it. He was just about
to put the receiver back on its rest when there was a
click, a voice: 'Hello? Hello? Who's that?'

'Dad?'

There was a brief silence. 'Matt . . . Thank God
for that. Jesus, Matt, you had us so worried. Your
mother called this afternoon to say you were OK.
Jesus, Matt. *Jesus*. Matt, are you there?'

'Sure, Dad, I'm here. I'm sorry. How's things?'

'Ticking over,' said his father. 'Same as ever. Well,
no . . . that's not true, is it? OK though. Listen,
we've got to talk, haven't we? Sort a few things out.
Fancy a trip up on Saturday? City are playing at
home, I think – fancy that? Hey, are you fixed up
with a team down there yet? That is, of course,
if you're planning to stay down there. Oh, Jesus,
Matt, I'm making a mess of this, aren't I? Are you
going to come up and see me? We'll sort everything
out, OK?'

'Sure, Dad. We'll sort everything out.'

Suddenly he became aware that he wasn't alone.

He looked up, certain that it would be Vince, or maybe Tina, come to gloat.

It was Kirsty. Watching him. Waiting for him to finish.

'Hey, Dad, I got to go, OK? I just thought I'd . . . you know, let you know. I'll call, OK?' He replaced the receiver, then reached up to put the telephone back on the chest of drawers.

He looked up at Kirsty, wondering how much she knew. She looked pale and nervous. Was she going to have one of her turns?

'You OK?' he asked.

She licked her lips and gave a brief nod.

'You know where I was, don't you?'

She looked genuinely puzzled, then her expression cleared. 'You were in my dreams,' she said. 'You called to me. You scared me.'

'I'm sorry,' Matt said gently. 'It was important. I couldn't have come back without your help. I'll always be grateful for what you did.'

'I keep dreaming,' she said. 'I can't stop them. It's frightening. The dreams are so much stronger now. They want me to help them, like I helped you. They want to break out.'

'But you beat them, don't you?' said Matt. 'Every time you have to beat them. Do you remember how you beat them? Remember the words Gramps taught you? The words that close the doors in your mind?'

She nodded. 'It's hard sometimes.'

'Of course it is,' said Matt. 'But you always win.

Because you're stronger than all those dreams. Do you believe me, Kirsty? Isn't that what Gramps would tell you?'

She smiled now. Suddenly, she rushed forward and hugged him. 'I'm glad you didn't stay in my dreams, Matt. It's not a very nice place.'

They'd moved Gramps along the ward, further from the door. Matt hoped that was a good sign. Someone had once told him that they kept the sickest ones by the door – that way they didn't have to keep wheeling the bodies out past the healthy.

Matt had hoped to see him up and out of his bed, but he was lying there, looking horribly weak. 'A little more poorly today,' the nurse had told him when he arrived at the ward.

'Gramps?'

At the sound of Matt's voice, his grandfather turned his head and stared at him. 'Matt,' he said. He opened his mouth, but no more words came.

'I'm back,' said Matt. 'I'm OK.'

'You've been . . .?'

Matt nodded. 'I've been there.'

Gramps looked shocked. 'I never knew it was possible,' he said. 'I never could. I never had your kind of strength. You have to be careful . . .'

Matt nodded and said, 'Kirsty helped me out. I've learnt a lot. I understand now.'

'You have to be careful, boy. You can't play games with it. It's too strong for that. You can't risk it spilling out. You *can't*!'

His grandfather's body arched upwards as he spoke. Matt looked around, half expecting to see a nurse rushing towards them. Nobody seemed to have noticed.

'I know, Gramps,' he said softly. 'I know what's at stake.'

'Why'd you do it? Why did you fool with it?'

Matt sat on the edge of the bed. 'I had to learn to control it,' he tried to explain. 'Vince –'

Gramps gasped at the name, then narrowed his eyes. 'Don't have anything to do with him, Matt, d'you hear me? His kind . . . they're drawn to the Way. It gets into their heads and they get all kinds of reckless ideas. They only . . . only cause trouble . . .'

Matt was sure his grandfather had been about to say more, but instead he stopped and his gaze became more distant. 'What is it, Gramps?'

Gramps looked at him again. 'Your grandmother took pity on him,' he said. 'She tried to help him be a better person. But he was full of it all by then. He tried to use her. He knew I was closed to him, and he knew I'd closed Kirsty to him. He thought your grandmother was a way through, but she wasn't. Eventually she saw him for what he was: a vessel of darkness whose only interest was in opening up the Way so that he could use its powers. He thought he'd be someone special with all that power at his disposal – the rest of us would have to respect him. We'd have to do anything he wanted. He didn't understand that it was just using him. Your grandmother tried to explain to him.'

'And?'

He shook his head. 'You know the rest, boy. I'm sure you know the rest.'

Vince was outside, working on his car again. From the other side of Bay Road Matt could see him, bent over the engine.

He crossed over and then turned down the street where his aunt lived. When he looked up again, the car's bonnet was closed and Vince had gone. Then he spotted him, sitting in the driver's seat with the window open, sucking on a cigarette.

Matt stopped by the passenger door and swung it open. He climbed in and slammed the door and, as he rolled the window down, he was aware of Vince's watching eyes.

'Thought I'd got you wrong,' his cousin said finally. 'Thought you weren't strong enough.' He smiled. 'Thought we'd lost you.'

'Why did you do it?' Matt asked. 'That vicar's nearly dead – he probably would be, if I hadn't found him when I did. You didn't have to do that.'

Vince tipped his head back and puffed a succession of smoke-rings into the air. 'He was snooping,' he said, when he had finished. 'Poking his nose in where it don't belong. I didn't want him messing things up for you, Matt. I was trying to protect you.'

'I don't need that kind of protection.'

'What was it like?'

Matt stared into the distance. 'Like . . . like nothing you can really imagine, but at the same time so *ordinary*. Like living in every nightmare you've ever had. You killed Gran, didn't you? You killed her because you couldn't use her.'

Vince's expression barely flickered. 'Life's tough,' he said. 'You have to make choices. Some of them aren't easy. She was the only one who ever trusted me, but then they turned her against me. That was her choice.'

'So you killed her.'

'I had an argument with her,' he said. 'Just the two of us. I raised my hand and she thought I was going to smack her one, but I couldn't. Not her. Not even then. But she *thought* I could. She fell down the stairs, trying to get away from me. She should have trusted me. She should have known I wouldn't hurt her. I only wanted her to help me.'

He took a cigarette out and lit it from the old one, which he then stubbed out on the back of the packet and flicked out of the window. 'We all have choices to make, Matt. You can't go changing them later. All that's in the past now, it doesn't count in the long run.' He turned to Matt, fixing him with his dark eyes. 'What matters is *you*, Matt. The things you can do, the powers you can set free. I want a part of it, do you understand? My whole life has been leading up to this point. The world's full of people who'll try to stop you making the most of your abilities. Busybodies who'll do all they can to interfere. I'll be your protector, I'll help you.

'You've had a taste of it, Matt. You, more than anybody, know the powers you can release into the world. Between us, we can control it.'

Matt sat back and closed his eyes. So much to take in. He had learnt to control his powers, but could he really learn to *use* them, too?

Vince was staring at him.

Who should he believe?

Matt remembered one of his first assessments of his cousin: the kind of person you would always want on your own side.

'I don't know,' he said. 'There's so much I don't know.'

Vince nodded grimly. 'So much to learn,' he said. 'And I'm offering you the time to learn it.'

It all changed again, later that evening.

They had eaten dinner in the familiar tense atmosphere, only lightened when Matt's mother raised the possibility of flat-hunting in the next few days. Tina, in particular, brightened up at that suggestion.

Afterwards, Matt went upstairs and changed into his tracksuit. He would go out for a run along the beach. It might help him exorcize a few mental ghosts, as well as prepare him for the new football season. It would give him a chance to think, a chance to get away from all this forced *niceness*.

He was on the bottom step when there was a loud knock at the front door.

He swung it open. A tall, dark-haired man was on the doorstep, standing with his hands at his sides.

Behind him were two more men. Matt recognized one of them as the detective sergeant who had come out to Crooked Elms that afternoon. The other man was a uniformed policeman.

The first man held out an ID card. 'Detective Inspector Stead, Bathside Police,' he said.

What more could they want, Matt wondered. He had answered all their questions in the afternoon. He had thought it was all sorted out.

The man was still talking.

'. . . to talk to Vincent Smith. Is he here?'

Matt glanced over his shoulder. Carol and Mike had appeared in the living-room doorway. 'Just missed him,' said Mike. He pointed out towards the street: there was a space where Vince's Ford Escort had been parked earlier. 'What is it? What's going on?'

'Where did he go?' Stead asked. 'It's important that we find him quickly. We have reason to believe he is a danger to the public.'

'What do you mean?' Mike demanded. 'What are you talking about?' He guided Carol out into the hallway, shutting the living-room door behind them.

Stead looked at each of them in turn, before resting his eyes on Mike once again. 'The Reverend David Walters died in Bathside General Hospital about half an hour ago,' he said carefully. 'He died from a blood clot resulting from the assault he suffered at your father-in-law's house in Crooked Elms. He regained consciousness briefly this evening and he was able to make a statement to one of my officers.

'Mr Smith, we want to talk to your son about the murder of the Reverend Walters. We want to talk to him very urgently indeed.'

17
GROWING APART

He didn't want to go to sleep.

He lay on his camp bed, staring at the shadows on the ceiling. Maybe if he had managed to go for his run, things would be easier. If he had run on that beach, and reassured himself that it was just a beach – if he had been able to draw the line between his experiences in Alternity and the real world – maybe now his head wouldn't fill with dark memories every time his eyes closed.

Some time later he heard a car pull up in the street outside. He rolled on to his side and squinted at his alarm clock. It was just after midnight.

He climbed quietly out of his bed and slipped across the landing to a small window that looked out over the street. Vince's red Escort was there, in its usual place.

The front door of the house opened and instantly a mutter of voices rose up the stairs. Mike must have been waiting for Vince to return.

Two floors up, Matt only caught snatches of their angry exchange.

'You must be joking, man!' Vince cried at one

point. Then, after more indistinct muttering: 'No way, man. They've got nothing on *me*. You must be out of your mind if you think . . .'

The front door opened, then slammed. From his vantage point Matt watched Vince stride across to his car and get in. The engine started, the headlights flared, and seconds later he was out of sight.

Matt returned to his camp bed and lay with his hands behind his head, staring up at the dark ceiling.

He doubted Vince would be back now: he would probably be driving away as fast as his old Escort would take him. It probably wouldn't be long before the police picked him up.

It made the situation a bit simpler for Matt, at least. It gave him some breathing space.

He turned over and closed his eyes. He hadn't slept for a whole week, he supposed. He couldn't put it off any longer.

He was getting the hang of Kirsty's racing game now. He could see how easy it was to get hooked on this kind of thing.

The two of them sat, side by side, on the living-room floor, alone, while Carol and Tina were working in the kitchen.

He felt remarkably well today. He didn't know if he had dreamed in the night: if he had, then no traces lingered when he awoke. The recent past was beginning to find some kind of perspective already. It was over, a set of experiences he had found his way through. Things seemed so much better in the daylight.

He returned the controls to Kirsty. She was still far better than him, and she never missed an opportunity to patronize him about it. 'Getting better,' she said now. 'At this rate you'll be able to dump the L plates in a week or two.'

He grinned and leant back against the sofa.

At the sound of the door opening he looked up.

Tina was glaring down at the two of them. 'Kirsty,' she hissed. 'I thought you wanted to help me with the bread.'

Kirsty smiled cheekily at her older sister. 'Me and Matt were just racing,' she said. 'You never play me at this one, but Matt will. He likes it.'

Tina's face coloured. 'Kirsty!' she snapped. 'I've *told* you. Now come through with me at once.'

Kirsty turned back to the television, ignoring her sister.

Tina came into the room and stood in her way. She bent over and grabbed her by the arms.

'Hey!' Kirsty squealed.

Tina's knuckles had whitened where she was gripping her sister.

Matt had seen enough. 'Go steady,' he said quietly. 'You're hurting her.'

Tina stared at him, easing her grip a fraction. 'What has it got to do with *you*?' she demanded.

She was nearly crying, he saw. The situation was out of her control. Matt was reminded of his escape from Alternity, when Kirsty had smashed a vase over her sister's head. *She never leaves me alone for long*, she had said then.

Tina didn't know how to leave her sister alone, he realized. For years now, Tina had established her role as Kirsty's protector, yet now Kirsty was growing up, becoming independent, Tina didn't know how to handle it. She didn't know how to let go.

He had been so intent on Tina that he hadn't noticed the effect this confrontation was having on Kirsty. Abruptly, she burst into tears. She shook Tina's hands off her arms and scrambled to her feet.

'Just leave me alone!' she cried. 'Stop it. Can't you see he's OK now? He's changed. It's all OK . . . can't you see?'

With that, Kirsty turned and fled from the room.

Tina stood dumbly, staring after her sister. Then she, too, burst into tears.

Matt looked away as she stood there, crying. Feeling awkward, he picked up the discarded handset and quit the game.

Finally, he pushed himself to his feet. 'She'll be OK,' he said softly. Again, he pictured the vase smashing down on Tina's head. He shrugged awkwardly, trying to blank out the image. 'Things could be worse, after all,' he added.

And pretty soon they were.

'Kirsty?' Carol had just poked her head around the door. 'Matt, have you seen Kirsty? She wanted to see the bread coming out of the oven.'

Matt looked up from his book. 'I think she went to her room,' he said.

A couple of minutes later, Carol came back, looking puzzled. 'She's not there,' she said. 'Tina's up there. She's been crying. She won't say why. Do you know what's been going on?'

How much should he say? 'They had an argument over the computer game,' he said, half-truthfully. 'About half an hour ago.'

Just then, Tina appeared behind her mother. Her face was pale, her eyes reddened from crying.

'Mum?' she said. 'What is it? Where is she?'

They exchanged worried looks.

Matt stood up. 'She's probably in the garden,' he said. 'It's a nice morning.'

The garden was deserted, apart from next door's Siamese, lying in a patch of sunlight, licking its paws.

They searched the house next, but she wasn't to be found.

'It's not like Kirsty to do something like this,' said Carol, for the third time. 'It's just not like her!'

It wasn't like Tina and Kirsty to argue, Matt thought, but they had.

'Right,' he said, trying to take control of the situation. 'She can't have gone far. She probably just wanted to be alone. She'll be back soon.'

'We have to look for her,' Carol said quickly. 'She's too young to be out like this. We have to find her. Just wait until I get my hands on her . . .'

Out in the street, they paused. Carol looked

all around. 'The roads . . . oh my God, the roads!'

'She'll be OK,' said Matt. 'Why don't you have a look around here – there are lots of places she could be.' Lots of alleyways and side streets. There were any number of routes she might have taken if she had decided to go into town for some reason.

'Tina,' he continued. 'Let's go down to the front. She's probably at that ice-cream stall by the beach huts. Did she have any money on her?'

They reached Bay Road and looked carefully in both directions. No sign of Kirsty. They crossed to the war memorial and looked down the left fork of the road, where it became Coastguards' Parade. There were more people in that direction, but none that looked like Kirsty.

'Come on,' said Matt, stepping into the road.

Tina started to cry again. 'It's my fault,' she said. 'It's all my fault.'

Matt shook his head. 'She's just growing up,' he said. 'You have to learn to give her a bit more space, that's all. It's no big deal, is it? Come on. The sooner we find her, the sooner you can patch it up, OK?'

Tina removed her glasses so she could rub at her eyes with the sleeve of her sweatshirt. Then she replaced them and followed him across the road.

They stopped at the railing, above where the grassy cliff tumbled gently down to the Promenade. It was cooler today than it had been recently, and there were fewer holidaymakers about: a few lazing on the grass, more strolling or chasing along the wide concrete Prom or playing on the beach.

There was a small knot of people around the ice-cream stall.

'Do you want to stick together, or should we split up?' Matt asked.

Tina straightened and said, 'We'll split up. It'll be quicker then.'

He left her walking along the top level in the direction of Eastquay. As he zigzagged down the path to the Promenade, he kept surveying the crowd but there was no sign of Kirsty. He tried to remember what she had been wearing: jeans, a pink flowery T-shirt, trainers.

He approached the stall from the side, jumping the queue.

'Excuse me,' he said, trying to catch the attention of the shaven-headed young man who was squirting soft ice-cream alternately into two cones. 'Hey, excuse me!'

The man looked up.

'I'm looking for a girl.'

'Aren't we all, mate? Only got ice creams here, though.'

'No, no . . . My cousin. Seven years old, mid-brown hair tied back. Glasses, jeans, pink T-shirt. She's gone off somewhere. Her mum's worried.'

The man shook his head. Matt turned to the people standing in the queue, but they were all looking blank, shaking their heads.

Matt backed away, turned, searched the crowd again.

For an instant he thought he had spotted her: a small girl, brown hair, pink top. But she turned, called out to somebody, and he saw that he was mistaken.

He searched for about a quarter of an hour, stopping people every so often to ask if they had seen her. They all looked blank, concerned. No one had seen her. He decided to turn back and see if Tina had been any luckier.

Just then, he spotted an old man leaning against the concrete wall that separated the Promenade from this part of Coastguards' Parade. He was watching the people as they passed, his eyes following them, studying them. Matt had seen him down here before, and put him down as some lonely old pensioner up from London for some sea air.

'Excuse me,' Matt said, approaching him. At first he had been self-conscious about approaching strangers, but now he scarcely gave it a thought. 'Have you seen a small girl? My cousin's gone missing and her mum's worried. Seven years old, glasses, mid-brown hair, jeans, pink T-shirt.'

The man shook his head.

But then he hesitated. 'You sure about the T-shirt?' he said. 'I saw a kid like that, about twenty minutes ago. Only she was wearing a black jacket, not a T-shirt.'

Kirsty had a black jacket. 'She could have had the jacket on over the T-shirt,' said Matt.

The man nodded. 'Suppose she could, couldn't she?'

'Where was she?'

The old man waved a hand towards the road. 'Over there. I noticed her because she was crying. Poor kid.' Then he straightened and smiled.

'Looks like you're wasting your efforts, though. She's already been found. I thought something like this had happened: I figured she'd been lost in the crowds and then she was found. Car stopped and she went over to it. Guy in the car was giving her a good telling-off, he was.'

'What happened?' asked Matt. 'Where is she now?'

'Got in the car, didn't she?' Suddenly, the old man looked concerned. 'It was a red Escort – that sound like the right car to you?'

Matt nodded. 'Yes,' he said grimly. 'That sounds like the right car, all right.'

18

OPENING THE WAY

'Hey! Come back!'

He hadn't planned it. It just happened. A man in shorts and vest, crouching to unchain his bicycle from the ornate iron lamp post. He had removed the chain from the bike's back wheel and turned to put it in his bag when, without hesitating, Matt swung his leg over the saddle and pedalled away as fast as he could.

He glanced back and saw the man sprinting after him, purple-faced with fury.

Matt pedalled harder. He didn't have time to stop and explain. He had been stupid to think Vince would just run away. What had Gramps said? People like Vince are drawn to the Way – it calls to them. Vince had seen the Way open, he had felt its power. Matt should have known he would try something like this! He had to get there as soon as possible. He had to get to Crooked Elms.

A short time later, he spotted Tina, walking along by the wall, searching the crowds for her sister. He jumped the bike up on to the pavement and cut a swathe through a group of startled pedestrians.

She looked up, surprised at the sight of him approaching on the stolen bike, then suddenly scared when she saw the grim look on his face.

'I know where she is!' he shouted. 'I'm going to get her back.'

When he glanced back, he saw the angry owner of the bicycle shouting at Tina, his cousin backing away from the man, frightened and confused.

He lowered his head and pedalled as hard as he could, dropping a couple of gears to climb the steadily rising road away from the bay.

He was hopelessly out of condition – if only he had kept up his football training through the summer! By the time he reached the first houses of Crooked Elms, he felt sick with exhaustion.

He came to the crossroads and swung right across the path of an oncoming van. Its horn blared at him but he didn't care. He was nearly there.

He approached the house and for an instant he thought he had got it wrong. Then he saw Vince's red car pulled up on the far side of the U-shaped drive. He swung his leg over the saddle and jumped off the bike, leaving it to crash, uncontrolled, into the hedge.

The house loomed over him. He closed his eyes and its presence lingered menacingly.

They were down there, he knew.

He just hoped he wasn't too late.

The front door was closed. Locked. He went to each of the front windows in turn and peered inside, but there was no sign of Kirsty or Vince. He went round to the side of the house. There was still a dark patch of blood on the ground where the vicar had been dumped.

He came to the back door and reached into his pocket for the key he had taken, the last time he was here. He slid it into the lock and it turned easily. Softly, he pushed the door open and went inside.

He listened, but there was nothing.

He knew they were here: he could feel it in his gut. He could feel the heat, the mental buzz. He could feel the disturbed energy coursing through the house.

He went through to the hallway. The door to the basement was closed, but it hid nothing from Matt.

He pulled it open and stepped inside.

The single bulb lit the basement. He looked down the steps and saw Kirsty lying in a corner with blood smeared across her white face – at first he thought she might be dead, but then she moved an arm and gave a little sob. Vince was standing in the shadows, his arms spread wide.

'Come *on*, you little cow! All you've got to do is say the words. Make it happen, Kirsty. Open it up!'

'No.' Matt didn't raise his voice, he just spoke in a normal tone, but it was enough.

Vince swivelled at the waist and stared up at him. Then he started to smile.

'Let her go, Vince,' said Matt. 'She's only a kid, for Christ's sake.'

'I can't, Matt. You know I can't. This is my

destiny, Matt. This is what I've lived for. It's in my head – I can feel it. It just needs to be set free! This is my chance to be in control, my chance to *be* somebody. We could be like kings, Matt. We could be like gods! You've tasted the power, Matt. You know what it's like. You're an outsider, just like me. You know I can't lose out now.' He grinned widely, madness in his eyes. 'It's gone too far for me to just let go.'

The Reverend Harold Allbright must have been like Vince: an outsider drawn to the power of Alternity. Obsessed by it. Corrupted by it. Until he had been defeated by Gramps.

Matt nodded slowly, aware of Kirsty's terrified eyes fixed on him. 'I know that,' he said. 'I know what it's like.' Then he pointed to Kirsty. 'But why the kid? Let her go, Vince. Let her go and I'll open the Way. I can do it. You know I can do it.'

Vince studied him carefully. Then he nodded. 'OK, then. Do it. But the girl stays here.'

Matt shrugged. 'She doesn't matter,' he said, coming down the stairs. 'She's only a kid.'

With each step, his feet became increasingly heavy. *Never the doors of the righteous be breached*, he recited, over and over in his mind, fighting the feeling, mastering it. He was in control. He could feel the power and he was in control.

He stopped close to Vince and met his look.

'Open it, Matt,' said Vince. 'Open it and keep it open, so the powers can break through. I want it. I want to use it.'

Matt nodded.

'Never the shield of our minds be breached,' he said, mixing up the words, scattering them at random, letting them come out in whatever order they chose.

'Shine shadow, where light had concealed!
Protect us from evil, protect us from fear.'

All the time, his eyes never left Vince's excited face.

'Shine shadow, where light had concealed!'

The air started to shimmer, blurring and distorting the pattern of bricks on the basement wall.

'Never the shadow, where light had concealed.'

He started to smile as he recited the words. The shimmering disc was taking form in the air. Just as before, the Way was opening up, about two metres in front of Matt.

Just behind Vince.

'Shine shadow, where light had concealed.'

He could feel it reaching out towards him, calling him.

He stepped forward and pushed Vince squarely in the chest.

Vince's mouth fell open in surprise and he staggered backwards.

Not far enough! Matt stepped forward and, before his cousin could steady himself, he pushed him again.

The shimmering disc rushed towards him, wrapping itself around Vince, swallowing him up.

In that fraction of a second, Matt had time to see the look of sheer rage that crossed Vince's features as he realized he had been tricked.

And he also had time to realize that Vince had grabbed him by the wrist and was pulling him with him, through the Way.

The shimmering disc wrapped itself round both of them, and Matt felt a sudden wave of heat and nausea swamping him, and then there was only blackness.

19

CLOSURE

He felt alone – more alone than he had ever been before – but he knew he wasn't.

He opened his eyes and saw himself in the distance, afloat in the blackness, adrift.

He managed to twist, to turn, and he saw another figure, turning, peering around, looking lost.

Only this time, it wasn't another version of himself. This time it was Vince. His pale, angry face was twitching and jumping as he tried to work out where he was, what was happening.

For a moment Matt felt guilty at having done this to his own cousin. But then he remembered Kirsty's terrified face, the sight of her features smeared with blood and tears in the dim light of the basement.

And the madness in Vince's eyes.

This had been his only chance to stop him.

Matt looked around again, and as he did so he made out the multiple versions of himself he had seen before, along with multiple Vinces, all angry, all confused. Some of them started to thrash about wildly, twisting and tumbling in the dark void.

What had he done? How had he got out of here before?

He closed his eyes and the darkness was complete. Calmness, absolute stillness. He was powerless here, he knew.

Running through endless, brick-walled corridors. Terrified of the dark presence in the shadows, in the depths of the maze, just waiting for him to make the wrong move.

He wasn't powerless any more, he knew. He could influence his own destiny.

But so could Vince.

And Vince was in here with him. He could hear his voice, screaming at him, threatening him.

He tried to pace himself, tried to think. The last time he was in this maze he had blacked out and woken up on the beach. Had that happened because he had been running for a certain amount of time, or had he passed on simply because he had stopped running?

He had to work it out. The only advantage he had over Vince was his previous experience.

He kept running. Kept running until his legs were like concrete and it was all he could do to drag one foot after the other.

The beach, sand and shingle pressing into his face.

As soon as consciousness returned, he was up on his knees, looking all around. He had to get away from here before Vince figured out what was happening. Because he felt certain that Vince would learn the ropes pretty quickly in a place like this.

'Hey! Come back!'

Vince was dragging himself out of the surf, bloody sea-water running down off his leather jacket.

Matt sprinted up to the Promenade and plunged through the staring crowd.

He had to get to Kirsty. He had to get out of here.

But in his haste he had forgotten about the others.

He swung the front door open and Vince was waiting for him, smiling, a claw hammer hanging casually from one hand.

Had Vince got here from the beach already, or was this one of the others?

It hardly mattered.

Vince raised the hammer and lunged at Matt.

He sidestepped and the hammer's metal head struck him on the shoulder, sending a stabbing bolt of pain right through his body. Vince was off balance and Matt pushed him into the wall, stunning him.

For an instant he thought about rushing into the house and taking his chance of finding Kirsty, but then he saw Carol advancing from the kitchen with a bread knife in her hand.

'Matthew,' she said. 'How lovely to see you.'

He backed away, then turned and ran.

*

Vince was coming along the street, his pale face smeared red from the beach. Matt turned and ran, back along the street towards an alleyway he knew would take him through to the main road.

Vince came after him, but then Matt heard his footsteps falter and stop. He looked back.

Vince was staring at his double in shock. Then he started to smile. He said something, and the two of them turned as one to look at Matt.

And then one Vince raised his hammer and smashed it into the other one's face.

The wet thud of the impact seemed to echo along the street.

Matt watched in horror as Vince's legs crumpled and he slid to the ground. The other Vince had to use both hands to pull the hammer out of his victim's broken face.

He knew he didn't have long. He didn't know how long it would be before Vince reappeared on the beach: a wiser, more experienced Vince.

He had to get to Kirsty.

He broke into a garden shed and armed himself with a hammer and a garden fork.

Back in the street, he approached his aunt's house, hoping desperately that Kirsty would be there and that his efforts weren't in vain.

Vince was still in front of the house, but the body had gone already.

He was swinging his hammer through the air, reliving his most recent triumph.

Matt came up behind him, taking him by surprise. He raised the fork with both hands and drove it down at Vince's back.

He thought at first that it wasn't going to sink in. The blow sent jarring vibrations right up the handle, and then abruptly the tines of the fork overcame the resistance and plunged into Vince's back.

A grunt emerged from Vince, and the fork was wrenched from Matt's grip.

Slowly Vince turned around, a look of surprise on his features.

Desperately, Matt reached for the hammer he had tucked into his trousers.

Vince stepped towards him, the fork still protruding from his back. He raised his own hammer, ready to strike, as Matt backed away. Vince swung, missing Matt by centimetres, and his momentum made him stagger forward on to his knees.

Matt stepped around him and rushed to the front door.

There was something odd about the house, something out of place. Then Matt saw what it was: a trail of mud across the carpet.

Carol was still in the hallway, arranging some dried flowers in a vase, as if she was merely finding something to occupy herself with while she waited for him.

She turned and smiled. 'Matthew,' she said. 'How lovely that you're here. There's someone waiting to meet you.'

He stepped past her into the living room.

From behind him, Carol continued, 'Yes, Matthew. The vicar has come to tea.'

Matt slammed the door shut behind him.

Kirsty was sitting on the floor exactly where he had hoped she would be.

And sitting in an armchair, sipping delicately from a cup of tea, was the Reverend Allbright. He was filthy, covered from head to toe in mud, and he had left a trail of soil across the carpet.

The Reverend Allbright caught Matt's eye and smiled, revealing the brown stumps of his teeth.

Kirsty stood up, a frightened look on her face. 'Reverend Allbright,' she said. 'He . . .'

The vicar rose, too. 'Matthew Wareden,' he said. 'How lovely to see you again so soon. Your grandfather was once so promising, but he lost his nerve, Matthew. He became scared. Maybe you will be different . . . You see, we want to get out of here. And either you or your cousin will help us. It really is that simple.'

He had something in his hand: something that glinted when the light caught it. Some kind of knife or chisel.

Matt had the hammer ready. He didn't have long. He swallowed and rushed across the room.

Allbright was prepared. He crouched low, waiting for Matt's attack.

Matt raised the hammer. 'Kirsty,' he said. 'I'm sorry.'

And then he swung the hammer down and smashed it into his youngest cousin's skull.

Sand and shingle in his face, the sound of waves, and mewing gulls scavenging debris from the sea.

He opened his eyes, made himself sit up. He blinked, trying to shut out the final image of Reverend Allbright's frenzied expression as he stabbed repeatedly down at Matt's face and neck.

Allbright hadn't understood. He'd known that Matt had tricked him, but he hadn't understood how. So violence was his natural response.

'Kirsty?' Matt called weakly. 'Are you here, Kirsty?'

His attention was drawn to a commotion along the beach. The tramp, staggering away as someone kicked at him.

Vince, Matt realized. Vince was attacking the tramp. He had forgotten Vince would have emerged on the beach just before him.

He rolled on to his knees to push himself to his feet. He had to get to Kirsty. It was his only hope.

'Matt?'

She was standing up to her ankles in the red surf, a hand raised to her head where he had struck her. She was crying, he saw. Scared.

'I'm sorry, Kirsty,' he said. 'I had to get you away from them. I need your help again. Do you understand? You have to get me out of here. You have to build the bridge again.'

She looked confused.

'The words, Kirsty. The magic words.'

She nodded. Licked her lips. 'Never the shield of our minds be breached,' she said hesitantly. 'Shine shadow, where light had concealed. Protect us from evil, protect us from fear . . . Is it working, Matt? Is that what you wanted?'

'Yes, Kirsty. Go on. Please don't stop.'

Up on the Promenade a crowd was forming: pale faces, bodies clothed in rags. They wanted to get out. They wanted to break out into the real world.

Among the crowd was a man dressed in black, a man who would lead them out: the Reverend Allbright was running straight down the grassy slope towards the beach.

'Shine shadow, where light had concealed.' Kirsty was scared. So was Matt: more scared than he would have thought possible.

'Come on, Kirsty,' he said. 'You're doing well.'

'Hey, you!' A shout from along the beach. Matt looked up and saw Vince starting to run towards them.

'Stop them,' Vince cried to the crowd. 'They're trying to trap us.'

Kirsty glanced along the beach.

'Go on, Kirsty!'

The crowd was surging down from the Prom, following Allbright. In a matter of seconds they would be on the beach!

'Never the shield of our darkness concealed . . . shine, shadow, shine!'

The air started to twist, the disc started to form.

Vince was sprinting now, running on the hard, wet sand.

The disc formed. Matt took Kirsty's hand and rushed at the Way, gasping as it reached out for them, swallowing them up in its embrace.

The last thing he heard was Vince's despairing wail.

He came to on the hard floor of the basement, exhausted, soaked with sweat.

He wasn't alone. He was holding Kirsty tightly in his arms.

Never the doors of the righteous be breached. The correct words, over and over in his head, fighting the rising blackness, the heaviness in his limbs. They had to get out of here.

He rose, still holding Kirsty, and carried her up the stairs to the hallway.

At last, he slumped and let her go.

She sat on the floor in a heap. 'What did you do?' she asked quietly.

'It's OK,' he said. 'We're OK.' Then he looked at her more closely. 'What is it?' he asked. 'What do you mean?'

'It's gone,' she said, glancing back at the basement door. 'You've closed it.'

But he could still feel it, the Way. It was only Kirsty who could not.

He smiled. He hadn't known if it would work:

all he had wanted to do was to get the alternative Kirsty away from Vince and the mad crowd on the beach. 'It's OK,' he said again. 'I just brought a part of you back from Alternity. You really can't feel it any more?'

She shook her head. 'It's gone,' she said. 'It really has gone.'

'You're the Guardian now,' Gramps told him, as the two of them sat together on the bench in the little hospital garden.

'I know,' Matt said quietly. He was the only one of his generation who could take on the role, now that Kirsty's sensitivity had been removed.

Gramps studied him closely. After a long interval he nodded and said, 'Yes, you do, don't you?' After another long pause, he added, 'You're strong. I can see that. You've grown. Does it frighten you?'

Matt nodded. 'It should do, though, shouldn't it? But I know I can handle it. I can beat it – or, at least, I can *contain* it. It feels good to know that.'

'Good. Our kind are the people who hold society together. We always have done. You're not alone, Matt. There are other Ways, other Guardians. You'll meet some of them, in time.'

Now Matt understood why Gramps had travelled so much in the past: he had not been fleeing his responsibilities at all – he had been meeting other Guardians.

'It's a good life, Matt. An *important* life. Your gran would have told you so, too. We can't all choose our own battles. Sometimes they choose us.'

Matt nodded, and he knew that everything was going to be OK.

EPILOGUE

Autumn sun flooded her bedroom, just as it had when she was a child.

Jill Guilder went across to the window and looked down on the U-shaped drive. She was just in time to see Matt ride off on his new bike with some of his friends, heading for football practice at Bathside School.

She sat down in the window seat and breathed deeply. She was learning how to be happy again, she realized.

It was a slow process, but at last life was starting to come together again.

After three months of temping, she had finally landed a permanent job. Gramps was improving all the time – in fact, now that he was back in his own home, he was almost back to his old self.

And Matt.

Matt seemed to be settling in. He seemed to like living in Gramps' house at Crooked Elms. And he got on so well with his grandfather – it made her feel guilty that they had visited so infrequently before.

He'd started at Bathside School in September, and he seemed to be adapting well. He visited his father in Norwich at regular intervals, and Nigel came down every Sunday to watch him play in the local youth team.

A couple of months ago she would never have believed things would work themselves out so quickly.

A couple of months ago . . . Was that all it was?

She recalled the panicked telephone call from her sister, telling her that Kirsty had disappeared, and then Matt had gone too.

She remembered the fear, the desperate searching.

She still didn't know how Matt and Kirsty had ended up at Crooked Elms. There had been a garbled explanation that had involved Vince, but she had known immediately that Matt was lying, or at least not telling her the whole truth. Even now, she wondered if it was fair to doubt him – Vince's car had been there at the house, after all.

But there had been no trace of Vince himself. No sign of him at all.

In fact, the only trace of Vince was in the dreams she had started having, shortly after moving in with her father. The dreams featured Vince and another man, who seemed to be some kind of clergyman. They seemed to be friends, the two of them. They seemed to be working together.

They were strange, disturbing dreams, ones she tried hard to forget as soon as she awoke.

It was only natural, she supposed. It was perfectly

normal to suffer nightmares after such a traumatic time.

Only natural that they should feature Vince.

Talking to her.

Calling to her.

Trying to find the doors in her mind . . .

*Another frighteningly good read
by Nick Gifford*

PIGGIES

Two sharp points of pressure on his neck.
Hard. Hurting. The sudden release as his skin
broke in two places. He cried out, but the sound
choked off in his throat. It hurt more than
anything he had ever known.

'A contemporary horror story to sink your
teeth into' – *The Times*

hotnews@puffin

Hot off the press!
You'll find all the latest exclusive Puffin news here

Where's it happening?
Check out our author tours and events programme

Bestsellers
What's hot and what's not? Find out in our charts

E-mail updates
Sign up to receive all the latest news
straight to your e-mail box

Links to the coolest sites
Get connected to all the best author web sites

Book of the Month
Check out our recommended reads

www.puffin.co.uk

For complete information about books available from Puffin – and Penguin – and how to order them, contact us at the appropriate address below. Please note that for copyright reasons the selection of books varies from country to country.

www.puffin.co.uk

In the United Kingdom: Please write to Dept EP, Penguin Books Ltd, Bath Road, Harmondsworth, West Drayton, Middlesex UB7 ODA

In the United States: Please write to Penguin Group (USA), Inc. P.O. Box 12289, Dept B, Newark, New Jersey 07101–5289 or call 1–800–788–6262

In Canada: Please write to Penguin Books Canada Ltd, 10 Alcorn Avenue, Suite 300, Toronto, Ontario M4V 3B2

In Australia: Please write to Penguin Books Australia Ltd, 250 Camberwell Road, Camberwell, Victoria 3124

In New Zealand: Please write to Penguin Books (NZ) Ltd, Private Bag 102902, North Shore Mail Centre, Auckland 10

In India: Please write to Penguin Books India Pvt Ltd, 11 Panscheel Shopping Centre, Panscheel Park, New Delhi 110 017

In the Netherlands: Please write to Penguin Books Netherlands bv, Postbus 3507, NL–1001 AH Amsterdam

In Germany: Please write to Penguin Books Deutschland GmbH, Metzlerstrasse 26, 60594 Frankfurt am Main

In Spain: Please write to Penguin Books S. A., Bravo Murillo 19, 1° B, 28015 Madrid

In Italy: Please write to Penguin Italia s.r.l., Via Felice Casati 20, I–20124 Milano

In France: Please write to Penguin France S. A., 17 rue Lejeune, F–31000 Toulouse

In Japan: Please write to Penguin Books Japan, Ishikiribashi Building, 2–5–4, Suido, Bunkyo-ku, Tokyo 112

In South Africa: Please write to Longman Penguin Southern Africa (Pty) Ltd, Private Bag X08, Bertsham 2013